Wedding

Season

By

Samantha

Chase

Prologue

Fifteen years ago…

Tricia Patterson nervously approached the closed classroom door. Her heart was beating wildly in her chest and she had to stop and take a few steadying breaths. This wasn't anything new. The way her family moved around, you'd think she'd be used to this by now.

New home.

New school.

And repeat.

Unfortunately, it never got any easier. The anxiety, the nerves, the fear of not fitting in. Most of the time it worked out all right. She'd make new friends, but in the back of her mind she knew it wouldn't be long until she had to pack up and move again.

But not anymore.

Thanks to her parents' divorce, Tricia wouldn't have to move again. She and her mom had found a place in a small town on the east coast of Long Island and they wouldn't have to pack up and move unless they wanted to.

She really hoped they wouldn't want to any time soon.

It had taken a couple of days to get unpacked and settled in, and today her mom had finally brought her to the local high school to get registered. Secretly, Tricia had hoped to drag out the process a little bit longer, but no such luck. She was here, registered, had her locker assigned and her schedule freshly printed out.

There was no turning back.

Looking down, she stared at the schedule for at least the tenth time in as many minutes. "It's just homeroom," she muttered. "Nothing to do except sit and wait until the first bell. You can do this."

With a steadying breath, she reached for the door, turned the handle and opened it.

Twenty-five pairs of eyes were instantly on her and her breakfast threatened to make a reappearance.

"May I help you?" the teacher asked. She was an older woman – maybe in her sixties – but she had a kind smile.

"Um…I'm Tricia Patterson," she said softly as she walked toward the desk. "I just transferred here and…" Reaching into her one binder, she pulled out her paperwork and handed it to the teacher.

"Welcome, Tricia. I'm Mrs. O'Keefe," she said, still smiling. "Why don't you take a seat for now? I'll rework the seating arrangement for tomorrow, but for now, feel free to sit at one of the empty desks."

"Thank you," Tricia mumbled and turned around. Okay, now there were only twenty-four people staring at her and it was still pretty damn intimidating. Scanning the room, she located an empty desk in the back corner, quickly made her way over and sat down.

After a minute, everyone seemed to lose interest in her and Tricia breathed a sigh of relief. She pulled out the papers they had given her down in the office and found a map of the school to show how to get from one class to the next. She was studying it when all of a sudden...

"Hey! I'm Sean Peterson."

To her right, there was a boy, Sean, leaning over smiling at her. She glanced at him and wasn't sure how to respond. Was he being nice? Sincere? Or was he someone she should avoid? Lord knows she'd dealt with that sort of thing in each school. It never failed that there was at least one person who seemed to genuinely want to befriend her only to turn out to be a freak in some way, shape or form.

"Hi," she muttered and went back to studying the map.

"So, you just transferred here? From where?" he asked.

Mentally she rolled her eyes. Placing the paperwork back down, she turned her head and looked at him. "From Rochester."

"Really? Upstate, huh? That's cool." He straightened and smiled and Tricia had to admit he seemed really nice. And he was kind of cute. Sandy brown hair, brown eyes and a nice smile. "When did you move?"

"Over the weekend," Tricia said but didn't know what else to add to her short response.

"Awesome. Where in town? I live over off of Barnford. I don't know if you know where that is but…"

"It's right by where we live, too," Tricia said, hating how she sounded so excited at the information. "I mean, we actually live on Barnford. The house on the corner of Barnford and Grove."

"Seriously?" Sean asked, his smile growing. "You mean the white house with the red shutters?"

Tricia nodded.

"I'm actually a block over," he said. "I'm on the opposite side of the street, on the corner of Barnford and Elm."

"No way!"

"Totally serious." He twisted in his seat so he was facing Tricia. "Do you have your schedule?"

She pulled it from her pile of papers and handed it to him. "This is the part I hate the most. Trying to find the classrooms and figuring out who to sit with."

"Well that's easy," Sean said. "Your schedule is almost identical to mine." He looked up at her again, his brown eyes smiling. "Just stick with me and I'll get you to all of them and then you can sit by me."

Tricia almost sagged with relief. "I...I appreciate it."

"There's just one problem," he said, his expression going almost comically serious.

"What?"

"I don't know your name. I mean, I know you said it when you walked it, but I didn't really hear it. I don't mind walking with you to classes, but I figure you'd prefer it if I didn't call you 'Hey, you' all day."

Tricia couldn't help but giggle. "I'm Tricia. Tricia Patterson."

Sean's smile was back. "It's nice to meet you, Tricia." Then he leaned in as if he had a secret to tell her. "With you being Patterson and my last name being Peterson, I think we're going to be stuck with each other all through high school. It's a good thing we became friends now."

And in that moment, Tricia couldn't agree more.

One

"You have *got* to be kidding me," Tricia grumbled as she sorted through the mail that was just delivered. She considered running down the block after her mailman and throwing it all back at him and shaking him until he promised to be more considerate, but then thought better of it. After all, it wasn't his fault she was a single woman.

A single woman who was currently holding three wedding invitations in her hand.

Cursing under her breath, she made her way back up the driveway and into her house, slamming the door behind her. Tossing the pile on her little entryway table without opening it, she walked through to the kitchen to get a drink. The sound of her phone ringing stopped her.

Her foul mood was instantly forgotten when she saw Sean's name on the screen. "Hey! It's you!"

"Hey, beautiful," Sean said with a small chuckle. "How are you doing?"

Walking into the living room, she collapsed on the couch. "Okay…and you?"

"By the sound of your voice, I'd say you are officially lying to me. So what's going on, Patterson?"

She rolled her eyes, hating how he rarely called her by her first name. "Three more came today."

8

"You're kidding!"

"Do I sound like I'm kidding?"

Sean chuckled again. "How is this even possible? How could it be that almost everyone we know is getting married this summer? Didn't they all get married last summer?"

"That's what I thought," she mumbled and threw her head back with a sigh. "I'm telling you, Sean, I'm nailing the mailbox shut as soon as we're off the phone!" The two of them had been commiserating over the last week about the upcoming wedding season.

"Tampering with the mail is a federal offense," he joked and Tricia couldn't help but smile.

"I'm not tampering with the mail, per se. It's my mailbox and if I want it nailed shut then…"

"Relax," he said smoothly. "Besides, how many more invites could there possibly be? I don't think we know any more people."

"I don't know. I have a feeling we're still missing some."

"Sure but…what are the odds of those people getting married this summer too? As it is, we're up to what? Five weddings? Six?"

"Today's mail brought us up to six."

"Yikes."

"Exactly." It really was a little more than Tricia wanted to deal with. She was feeling like the proverbial "always a bridesmaid, never a bride" while Sean had complained about how he was tired of people trying to set him up with their "cute" sisters or cousins. "Seriously, we don't have to go to all of them, do we?"

"I mean I guess we don't have to," Sean began, "but...they are all our friends. Whose would we skip?"

Standing, Tricia quickly went over and grabbed today's invitations and then walked to the kitchen to grab the three that had arrived the previous week before sitting back down on the sofa. "Okay, let's think about this. The first one is Tami and Eric on June third." She paused. "Actually, I'd really like to go to that one. They're a great couple and have always been good friends to me."

"Ditto," Sean said. "Next?"

"Linda and Jerry on the fifth. Wow. It's going to be a very full weekend."

"Yeah, but...if we do one, we kind of have to do the other. It will be all the same people and how would we explain going to one and not the other?"

"Good point," Tricia conceded. "Give me a minute to open these new ones and see if any of the dates overlap."

"Wishful thinking, Patterson. Our luck is never that good."

"You know, I can't help but notice how you keep talking about all these events in the plural sense. Does that mean you're definitely going to be back home for the summer?"

"That's the plan," Sean said, and Tricia could hear the smile in his voice. For the last year, Sean had been working as a contractor over in the Middle East and Asia, helping to rebuild areas that were torn apart by war and a tsunami. It was hard work but she knew Sean loved it.

"And you want to spend your free time when you finally get home going to weddings? Seriously?" she asked with a laugh. "What's wrong with you?"

"Well, although it will cost me a fortune, it's a great opportunity to see everyone at one shot and get caught up."

It made sense. "Okay, next up we have…Donna and Jason on…" She scanned the invitation, "the eleventh. That's almost too much, right? Can we skip that one?"

"You can, but I can't. Jason and I played soccer together since we were five. I have to be there."

"Are you sure you're even invited? How often do you check your mail?" She asked with as serious of a tone as she could manage, but Sean knew immediately she was teasing.

"Ha-ha, very funny. I get my mail on a regular basis and although I haven't gotten today's mail – and probably won't until next week – I'm fairly certain I'm invited to all the same weddings as you."

"Fine, whatever. Don't get all defensive." She shuffled through the mail and opened up the rest of the invites. "It looks like we get a break for a couple of weeks and the next batch doesn't start up again until the second week of July."

"So that means we don't have to make any firm decisions right now then."

"You don't, but I do. The first one up in July is Kristen and Bobby. I told her I couldn't commit to being in the bridal party but that I'd be there."

"Okay, fine. Bobby was also on the soccer team so I should be there too."

"You know high school was over ten years ago, right? It doesn't matter that you played on a team together – it doesn't obligate you to stuff for the rest of your life," she said.

"You wouldn't understand," he replied. "We were all close and once I started traveling, I've missed out on a lot. My friends mean a lot to me – you should know that – and as much as it pains me to have to dress up and do the chicken dance, I want to be there for my friends."

Suddenly, Tricia didn't feel quite as antagonistic toward the invitations. "You're right," she sighed. "I guess there's a part of me that just dreads all that goes with accepting the invites."

"You mean the inevitable attempts to fix you up with someone?"

"That and the pity looks I get. And I get a lot of them. You know…the old 'Poor Tricia. You'll find someone soon. I'm sure of it.' I hate those looks."

"Yeah well, I'd take pity over pimps."

She couldn't help but laugh. "Is that what we're calling it now?"

"Might as well. It's pretty much what they're doing," Sean said and then sighed loudly. "I don't know maybe it's not…" He stopped. "Wait a minute," he began excitedly. "I've got it! I know exactly how to get us out of those situations!"

"I'm listening…" she said hopefully.

"We go together."

All of the hope she was just feeling quickly deflated from her body. "That's it? That's your big plan? How is that going to get us out of anything? Everyone is used to seeing us together. And considering you've been out of the country for so damn long, they'll just figure you didn't have time to find a date and so you asked me. I'll be the pity date!" She cursed. "Damn it! I can't escape it!"

"No, no, no…listen. We go together as like, you know, a couple."

She shook her head. "No one is going to believe it."

"Sure they will. We'll get all cozy and you'll have to look at me as if you adore me – which shouldn't be hard to do – and hang on my every word."

"You're crazy, you know that? I'm not going to hang on your every word and whatever else. It's ridiculous and it won't work."

"Why not? You're telling me you can't pretend to be in love with me for a couple of hours? I'm crushed."

"Don't be such a drama queen, Sean," she said wearily. "It's not just a couple of hours. We're looking at potentially six weddings at six-to-eight hours each with people who've known us for years. It's going to take a lot more than batting my eyelashes at you while holding your hand."

"What have we got to lose?" he asked. "Unless…unless you had someone else you planned on going with."

Unfortunately, she didn't. It had been months since she'd even been on a date. But there was no need to dwell on it right now. "No, that's not it. I just don't think…"

"C'mon, Tricia. It makes perfect sense. We'll test out the theory at the first wedding and see how it goes. I'm sure no one's going to expect us to be pawing at each other to prove we're in a relationship. What do you say?"

"I still think you're crazy but…"

"Look, it's not that big of a deal and I guarantee you we'll have a lot more fun this way. We'll shock everyone and then field all kinds of questions and then we'll get to enjoy ourselves. No ducking behind potted plants or running into the bathroom to avoid the feeding frenzy of well-meaning people who claim only to be thinking of our happiness."

Tricia took a minute to think about it and as much as she believed they'd never be able to pull it off, it was certainly worth a try. "You're right. Damn it."

"Excellent!"

"So that leads me to our other order of business, where you'll be staying while you're home. I hope it's here." Tricia was actually renting Sean's childhood home. From the first time she had walked through the front door, she had fallen in love with it. When Sean's mom wanted to move away and travel a bit herself, she had offered it to Tricia. Someday she hoped to own it but wanted to wait until the time was right.

"I wouldn't dream of staying anyplace else," he said. "Where else could I go for free and sleep in my old room?" He paused. "You haven't changed anything in there, have you?" he asked with exaggerated anxiety.

"No, precious," she mocked. "Your Van Halen posters are still on the wall so you can relax. I'll just have to unlock the shrine and air it out before you get here. Which reminds me, when exactly will you be getting home?"

15

"End of May. I'm thinking the twenty-eighth but figure you'll have to give or take a day with that. Nothing ever goes as planned."

"And what about your mom? Are you going to go and see her first and then come here or the other way around?"

"Honestly? I'm not sure. Probably after the first round of weddings I'll track her down. Last I talked to her she was going on a cruise with some friends and was talking about yoga classes." He sighed. "Why can't she just be like other moms?"

That made Tricia laugh. Stephanie Peterson had never been like other moms – that was one of the things she'd always loved about her. "You have no idea how lucky you are. Steph gets out there and is enjoying her life. My mom prefers to live like a hermit."

"That's not true and you know it," Sean said.

"Which part?"

"Your mom and John are very happy and they have plenty of friends. You need to stop picking on them."

"Hey, same goes for you, buddy. Your mom is very happy and has a lot of friends. She just chooses to have them all over the world. There's nothing wrong with that."

"I guess," he grumbled. "It's just hard to pin her down sometimes. It would be nice to have a home base to go and see her. I'm never sure where I'm going to find her."

"It's not like you've been home a whole lot, Sean," she reminded him. "I don't see why it should bother you so much."

"Yeah, well, it doesn't just bother me. Ryan complains about it too. Every time I talk to him he tells me how it's easier to find Waldo than it is to find Steph."

"Yeah, well...Ryan's just grumpy. I swear, he's always got something to complain about." It was only partially true. Ryan was Sean's older brother and while he and Sean had a great relationship, any time Tricia was around him he seemed to be irritated.

Sean chuckled. "I don't know where you get it from. Ry's not like that. He does his own fair share of traveling but even with that, Steph has him beat."

"I think that's great for her!"

"You women. Always sticking together."

"And don't you forget it." There was a moment of companionable silence before Tricia spoke again. "So you really think you'll be coming home this time?"

"I do. I know I said that six months ago but then the tsunami hit. I was already over here with a team. What was I supposed to do?"

"You don't have to fix the entire world, Sean. You have people back here who love you and want to see you."

"Aww...see? You love me. It's going to be so easy for you to play the part of my girlfriend for these weddings!" he teased.

"You're an idiot," she laughed.

"Yes, yes, yes," he agreed. "But you still love me."

That just made her laugh harder. "Knock it off, doofus."

"Come on. I'm not completely hideous to look at, am I?"

"Now you're just fishing for compliments. And besides, you've been gone for like two years. For all I know you could look like some kind of yeti now."

"I promise to shave," he said with a laugh. "Admit it. This is going to be so much fun. We can watch all of their shocked faces and we can be as outrageous as we want."

"I'm sure I'm going to regret this at some point, but okay. Fine. I guess it could be kind of fun. Plus, we'll get to spend a whole lot of time together getting caught up."

"So...it's a plan?"

She nodded even though she knew he couldn't see her. "Definitely. I'll take care of all the RSVP'ing for us if you don't mind."

"Be my guest, *sweetheart*," he gushed.

"*Ugh*...knock it off. Save it for the audience."

"You're no fun. How are we supposed to come off as being believable if we don't practice?"

"Sean?"

"Yeah?"

"Let it go. We'll be fine and I don't think either of us is going to have to pull off an Oscar-worthy performance."

"You never know..."

Tricia didn't even want to think about it. All she knew was her best friend was coming home and they'd have a couple of weeks to hang out together. Weddings or no weddings, it was going to be fun.

Two

Several things hit Tricia at once as she pulled into her driveway a month later. First, it was too hot to cook. Second, there was bird poop on her windshield so she was going to have to wash her car. And lastly, there was a strange car in her driveway.

"Sean!" she instantly squealed as she parked and climbed out of the car. He had mentioned he wouldn't be home until the end of May and that was still a few weeks away but...who else would it be? He probably just wanted to throw her off so he could surprise her.

Grabbing her purse, she closed the car door and practically ran up the front steps of the house. Sean still had a key so no doubt he was inside already. She let herself in, dropped her things in the doorway, and went looking for him.

No sign of him in the living room.

No sign of him in the kitchen.

Tricia was about to turn and walk up the stairs to look in his room when she caught sight of him through the French doors that led out to the deck. For a minute, all she could do was stop and stare. He was here, really and truly here. He looked bigger, taller, like he had filled out from all his time in construction. His brown hair looked kissed by the sun but could definitely use a trim, she thought with a smile.

With a contented sigh, she decided she'd be the one to surprise him by sneaking up on him. He may have heard the car, but it wasn't enough to make him come inside to investigate. Toeing off her shoes, she tiptoed through the kitchen and over to the doors. He looked completely at peace, although that could have something to do with the yard. Steph had been a whiz with the landscaping and gardening and she had really created something special back here.

An oasis.

At least that's what Tricia thought of it. With the Koi pond and lush foliage, it was something out of a magazine. And it was hers now – sort of. Tricia was certain that after all of the horrors Sean had witnessed in the last several years, this space must really seem like a little bit of heaven to him. It almost seemed a shame to disturb him but…she needed to. She needed to hug him, to see his face and make sure he was real.

In her best stealth mode, she quietly walked through the open doors and out onto the deck and didn't stop until she was directly behind him. He was standing on the edge of the deck looking down at the fish. Part of her wanted to be playful and yell "Gotcha!" but the softer side – the side that was just so happy to have him home – won out. Reaching out, Tricia simply wrapped her arms around his middle and rested her head on his back.

"I'm so glad you're finally here," she said softly as she squeezed. He cleared his throat and Tricia stiffened and pulled away before taking a step back.

"Hey, Tricia."

Apparently someone wanted to surprise her, but it wasn't Sean.

It was Ryan.

He had heard the car pull up.

He had known he'd have to see her.

But being touched by Tricia? Um, yeah. That wasn't something he'd counted on.

Slowly he turned around and faced her. And smiled. Everything about Tricia Patterson was familiar and yet looking at her right now, different. From the copper-colored hair to her green eyes, she was the girl he remembered. But taking in the rest of her? Well, she wasn't a girl any more. She had most definitely blossomed into a woman.

Ryan tucked his hands into the front pockets of his jeans and took a steadying breath. "How have you been?"

Her smile had only faltered slightly when she realized it wasn't Sean she was hugging and now - even though she was still smiling - he could see the apprehension there. "I'm fine. Fine. Um...how about you?"

He nodded. "I'm good." Ryan looked around the yard and knew this peaceful reprieve was over. "You're probably wondering what I'm doing here."

She blushed and ducked her head a little. "Well...yeah. I think the last time I saw you was..."

"About six years ago," he finished for her. "At Sean's graduation."

"Right," she said softly and then looked toward the house. "I'm sorry, where are my manners? Can I get you something to drink?" But before Ryan could answer, Tricia was walking back into the house.

He followed and found her in the kitchen. "I wasn't expecting anyone so I'm afraid I don't have a lot to offer – water, Coke, orange juice…"

"I'll take a Coke," he said, even though he wasn't particularly thirsty. Standing back, he watched Tricia flutter around the kitchen pouring their drinks. When she handed the glass to him, her eyes barely met his. "I probably shouldn't have just let myself in," he finally said to break the silence.

"What? Oh, no…it's fine. I told your mom when she rented the place to me that it's still your family's home. I'm just borrowing it for a while."

"Still…you had no idea I was coming, but I didn't know when you'd be home."

"You could have called," she said and glanced at him through her lashes.

Ryan nodded and placed his glass down on the counter. "Look, Tricia, this isn't really a social call. Which – ironically – is why I didn't call."

She paled and placed her own drink down next to his. "What's going on?" she asked nervously. "Is it your mom? Sean?"

Shit. He hated doing this, hated being the messenger and delivering bad news. "Why don't we go and sit down?" he asked quietly and went to reach for her arm to guide her out to the living room.

"Just tell me," she said, taking a cautious step back. "Please, Ryan." There was a tremble in her voice and it affected him more than it should have.

He sighed with resignation. "There was another storm," he said lowly, watching her face as his words sank in. "It hit in the middle of the night. No one saw it coming."

Tricia's body slowly began to sag to the floor. Ryan tried to reach out and catch her, but all he managed to do was sit down on the ceramic tile beside her. Tricia's green eyes filled with tears as she looked at him. "Sean?" she whispered.

"It's too soon to tell. Mom got the call and then called me. We've been trying to get someone to talk to us but it's chaos over there."

"I...I don't understand," she said as the tears began to fall. "How...? Why...?"

Ryan wrapped an arm around her shoulders – it seemed like the thing to do. "I was out east when I got the call. I had some business out there and I was going to just head back to Jersey and see what I could do, but mom mentioned she was going to call you and I just thought..." He shrugged. "I thought this was something you should hear in person."

It was clearly the wrong thing to say because her expression crumbled and the next thing Ryan knew, Tricia was sobbing hysterically against his shoulder.

"No…no," he said, trying to tuck a finger under her chin to get her to look at him. "We have to stay positive. Just because we haven't heard anything doesn't mean something's happened to Sean."

He only wished he believed it.

"I just…well…I know how close you and my brother are and I felt like it was better if someone was here with you."

Tricia nodded and looked up at him. "What about…where's Steph? Is she okay?"

It always amazed him how Tricia's first reaction was to always think about others. For as long as he'd known her, he found that to be true about her. "She's upset and worried but she's in Palm Springs surrounded by her friends and for now…she's okay."

Quickly climbing to her feet, Tricia stood and immediately walked out of the kitchen. Ryan followed after her. "What are you doing?"

"I should call her," she said, scanning through her contacts before hitting send. She looked over at Ryan. "I just want her to know I'm here for her."

Unable to help himself, Ryan smiled. How was it that not thirty seconds ago this woman was on the floor crying her heart out and now she was going to offer her support to his mother? Not wanting to eavesdrop on the conversation, he walked back to the kitchen.

When his mother had called him, the first thing he'd felt was dread. Then anger. He hated that Sean was constantly putting himself in harm's way by working in such a dangerous region. Sure it was admirable work, but there were plenty of ways he could put his skills to work here at home.

With him.

Hell, he'd been after Sean to go into business with him since he graduated! Between Ryan's architecture skills and Sean's building ability, they could do great things together. But Sean wanted to go out and help the masses, the world – be anyplace but here.

And now what? Didn't Sean realize there were people here who cared about him? Worried about him? Hell, Ryan had started making calls as soon as he'd gotten off the phone with his mother. When he realized with the time difference and the magnitude of the damages over in the Philippines that he wasn't going to get anywhere, his first instinct had been to go home and be by himself.

And then his mother had mentioned Tricia.

Even now Ryan couldn't say why he felt the need to come here and tell her himself. He meant what he said to her earlier about how he didn't think she should be alone when she heard, but that didn't mean he had to be the one here with her. And yet…who knows? Maybe on some level he needed to be here.

This was his childhood home. He felt a connection to Sean here that he couldn't find anyplace else.

With a shaky hand, he reached for his drink and walked back out to the deck. He remembered all the work his mother had put in back here. After his father had died, working in the garden had been one of the few things that had brought her joy. Tricia had done a great job keeping up with it – no doubt it was a full-time job in itself.

Several minutes had gone by when he heard her come outside. Looking over his shoulder, he saw she looked a little more at peace. "How'd it go?"

Tricia took a shuddery breath. "Like us, she's scared and worried and just wishes someone would call and give her an update." She stood beside him and looked out at the yard. "I told her you were here and she said she would probably be heading back this way soon too."

Ryan nodded. There was nothing they could do right now but wait. He'd done what he said he'd do – he came and broke the news to Tricia in person. Looking at his watch he saw it was a little after six. If he got in the car now, he could be home before nine. The thought of driving wasn't all that appealing but at least he had missed most of the evening traffic.

"I think I'm gonna hit the road," he finally said and finished his drink. "It's a long drive and it's been a long day."

"Oh," Tricia said softly. "I...I guess I just thought you'd stay here tonight. There's plenty of room." Then she chuckled. "Actually, there's your room."

Ryan couldn't help but chuckle too. It was a very appealing offer. He was tired and more than a little distracted. Maybe it wouldn't be the worst thing for him to do tonight.

"Are you sure?" he asked. "I don't want to impose."

She smiled. "Are you kidding me? The thought of being alone after learning all of this will just have me probably sitting in the dark and crying. Please stay." She paused. "I…I'd really appreciate it."

Ryan turned his head and looked at her and smiled back. "Thanks. I'd like that too."

****

Ryan Peterson was four years older than Tricia and Sean and by the time she and her mom had moved up the block, he had already graduated from high school. Tricia really only saw him when he was home from college during breaks and even during those times, it wasn't very often.

He was much more serious than Sean ever was and Tricia always had the feeling she annoyed him. True, that was a long time ago and they were both adults now, but that didn't stop her from feeling a little awkward with him.

A small breeze blew and the first few sprinkles of rain began to fall. "I don't remember hearing rain was in the forecast," Tricia said as they walked back into the house, shutting the French doors behind them.

Ryan simply nodded and went to place his glass in the sink. Tricia studied him for a moment – now that she knew it was him, she couldn't believe she had actually thought he was Sean earlier. For starters, he was taller – easily six feet if not more. And where Sean was always a bit thin and wiry, Ryan was a bit more…solid and muscular. He was dressed casually in well-worn blue jeans, a black t-shirt and work boots and there was a definite five o'clock shadow shading his strong jaw.

He turned and caught her staring. "You look great, Trish," he said as he seemed to equally appraise her as she'd just done to him. After a minute he turned and began walking around the house. "I can't believe how much everything still looks the same around here. I thought for sure you would have changed some things around."

"Are you kidding?" she asked with a laugh. "This house is amazing. I've always loved it. All of the furniture is so comfortable and other than putting up some personal stuff, like my pictures and whatnot, I can't imagine changing a thing."

He looked at her and laughed too. "Are you just saying that because it's me? I would imagine if mom actually sold you the place you'd make some changes."

She shrugged. "Maybe. I mean, the only room I really made my own was the master bedroom. Other than that, it's all your family's stuff. I was just joking with Sean not too long ago how your bedroom is still intact. All of your posters are still up on the wall and…"

And then it hit her.

Sean.

Ryan must have sensed what she was thinking because he was immediately at her side, his hands on her shoulders. "Hey," he began softly. "Come on. None of that." He looked around the room. "Seriously. Everything looks wonderful. You're taking good care of my house." He winked at her before removing his hands and taking a step back.

"Your house, huh? Any chance of you sticking around long enough to clean out your gutters?" She was teasing but Ryan immediately jumped into action.

"Sure. Is there a ladder out in the garage? I can easily…"

"Ryan, I was just kidding!" she chuckled. "Besides, it's raining, remember?"

"Oh…yeah. Right. Anyway, I can definitely do that for you tomorrow."

"It's really not a big deal. Honest. I was just goofing around."

With a nod, Ryan looked around the rest of the main floor. Tricia walked along with him. It wasn't a large house – a three bedroom Cape Cod – but for her, it was the greatest house she'd ever lived in. To her, this house represented a happy family, something she didn't have growing up. Once she and Sean had become friends, she'd spent a lot of time here and all of her memories were good ones.

"Are you hungry?" she asked before Ryan started up the stairs. She didn't feel the need to go and tour his old bedroom with him. "I hadn't planned on cooking tonight but I could very easily call in for pizza or something."

"That actually sounds good," he said. "Unless you want to go someplace? I wouldn't mind checking out some of the old local restaurants."

"Are you sure? I know you hadn't planned on any of this…"

"I think you know enough about me to know I wouldn't have offered if I wasn't serious, Tricia." His voice was firm but there was a glimmer of humor in his eyes. "Besides, I think it might be good for both of us to get out for a little while. And I'll have my phone with me – just in case."

She nodded. "Okay. I'll be honest. I can't even remember the last time I actually went out someplace for dinner. It's usually just me and the bag of takeout." She realized how depressing that sounded but didn't think it would help if she tried to take it back.

It wasn't as if this was the life she actually wanted, but it was what it was. By now she had imagined herself being married and with a couple of kids. Instead, she was single and worked from home. Working as a speech pathologist was something she loved and found very rewarding. Working with kids and making a difference with them was something she always dreamed of.

She just needed to remember to make some time for herself.

"I dine out a lot with clients," he said with a shrug, "but it's been a while since I've just gone out with a friend."

Aww...she thought to herself. "Why don't you bring your stuff in and get settled in. You can use the guest room down here or your old room. The choice is yours. And let's say...thirty minutes? Then we'll go?"

"Sounds like a plan," he agreed.

Tricia walked up to her room as Ryan went out to his car. A minute later she heard him climbing the stairs, obviously choosing to sleep in his childhood room. The upstairs of the house only contained the two bedrooms and a shared bath so it would be a bit of close quarters for the time being.

Sitting on the bed, she couldn't help but look around. It truly was the only room she had changed since moving in and she loved it. There were large windows, a skylight and it was so bright and airy. The only real piece of furniture in the room was her bed. The rest of the room consisted of built-ins and bookcases – all of which were filled to capacity.

She heard Ryan moving around in his room and wondered what he must be thinking. It seriously did look exactly as it had when he and Sean lived here. She didn't need the room and at first it had been a bit of an ongoing joke to leave it as a shrine, but then time just got away from her and out of all the rooms in the house, it was the one she needed the least.

And so a teenage boy's room it stayed.

It actually reminded Tricia more of a cave than a boy's room – dark paneled walls, dark wood furniture, navy blue bedding – and it didn't have half the windows Tricia's room did. Luckily she wasn't the one who had to live or sleep in there. Whenever Sean came to visit, however, he seemed to take great joy in staying in there. Hopefully Ryan would too.

They met out in the hallway not much later, both ready to go. Before she could step down the first step, Ryan said her name and stopped her. She looked at him curiously.

"Thank you," he said.

She couldn't help but smile. "For what?"

"For giving me the gift of being able to come home again," he said, his voice a bit gravelly. "I really needed this. More than I realized. So…thank you."

Unable to help herself, she stepped forward and hugged him. That was twice in one day she had ever touched Ryan and it felt really good both times.

Tricia knew how both Ryan and Sean hadn't wanted their mom to sell the house – and she couldn't blame them. But Steph had felt it was too big for her and wanted to travel without the responsibility of a house. Renting it out to Tricia had seemed like the perfect solution – it was why she always promised they could come and visit any time. It was good to see she'd made the right decision.

With one last squeeze, Tricia stepped back and looked at him, happy to see how he looked a lot more relaxed than he had a little while ago. "Now, how about that dinner?"

Three

It was after ten when they got back to the house. Dinner had been wonderful and surprisingly, the conversation never let up. Tricia knew she hadn't laughed that much in a long time.

She heard him close and lock the front door as she walked through to the kitchen. "Can I get you anything?"

Ryan strolled in behind her. "I know it seems crazy after all we just ate but…do you happen to have any ice cream?"

Her smile grew.

"What? What are you smiling about?"

"Clearly you don't know me very well if you even have to ask about ice cream. It's the one staple I keep in the house." Walking over, she pulled the freezer door open. "We have the basics – vanilla, chocolate, and strawberry – but then I also have cookie dough and chocolate chip."

He chuckled and came to stand beside her. "Would it be wrong to want a little bit of each?"

"Not at all." They worked together to make up their own dessert and as Tricia was putting everything away, she noticed Ryan looking at her wall board covered in invitations.

"What's all this?" he asked.

Rolling her eyes, she took a spoonful of ice cream before answering. "That," she began, "is my own personal hell."

He chuckled. "No. Seriously. What are all these?"

Tricia stepped up beside him and sighed. "These are wedding invitations. So far I've been invited to six of them this summer."

"Six?" he asked incredulously. "Seems a bit excessive to me. You're not going to all of them, are you?"

She nodded. "Actually, Sean and I are going together. We…" And then she stopped. Wave after wave of sadness washed over her and it was all she could do to put the bowl down on the counter and not fall to the floor again.

"Trish?" Ryan said softly. "Positive thoughts, okay?"

She shook her head this time. "I feel so guilty," she said, her voice a mere whisper.

"Why?"

"We're sitting here having ice cream and laughing and having a good time and we have no idea if Sean is okay! It's not right!"

Placing his bowl down beside hers, he took her by the hand, led her out to the living room sofa and sat down with her. "I have to believe he's okay," he said after a moment. "I have to believe the phone lines are down and that once things are up and running again, Sean's going to call and say everything is all right. Sitting here crying and thinking the worst isn't helping anyone."

She studied him. "I know you're right but I can't help but feel bad and…"

"Tell me about the weddings," he interrupted. "Tell me how it is that the two of you are going together. How did that come about?" Then he stood and went to grab their desserts and brought them back to the living room, sitting back down beside her.

For the next few minutes, Tricia told him about the pact she and his brother had made, chuckling by the time she was done. "I still can't believe I agreed to it. But the thought of everyone looking at me like they feel sorry for me was more than I could handle."

"I doubt anyone would look at you that way."

"Trust me. They do and it's awful." She took another couple of bites of her ice cream. "And poor Sean…people were always trying to set him up with someone – even if he came with a date! I'm telling you, when people are involved and in love, they want everyone to be too."

"That's not a bad thing."

"Oh yeah? Have you gone to any weddings lately?"

He shook his head. "I avoid them like the plague."

37

She eyed him suspiciously. "Probably for all the same reasons I just mentioned, right?"

He chuckled. "Guilty."

Tricia sighed and rested her head back, her ice cream finished. "He was so excited about going to these things," she said sadly. "We talked about it and talked about it and he thought he found the perfect solution. He told me I'd have to play the adoring girlfriend."

Ryan sat back beside her, their heads almost touching. "And you didn't want to?"

She shrugged. "I just didn't think anyone would believe us. Everyone knows we've been friends forever. It would be hard to convince them that suddenly we're dating and in love."

"Maybe. Maybe not." He paused. "But if anyone can pull it off and schmooze a crowd, it's my brother."

Then they both chuckled and grew silent. Sean Peterson was one of those guys who was everyone's friend and had no enemies. Tricia knew Ryan was right – somehow Sean would be able to convince everyone of anything he put his mind to.

She just hoped and prayed he would come home and prove her right.

Ryan sat up and stood. Without a word, he took her empty bowl from her hands and brought it into the kitchen. He returned a minute later. "I thought I'd be exhausted by now, but I'm more awake now than I was when I got here. Want to watch a movie or something?"

"That sounds good." Tomorrow was Friday and she had the day off. It was a lucky coincidence. She had planned on working on lesson plans for her clients and doing some research on new therapy options but knew she could still do those things if she stayed up late tonight.

"I'm actually going to go upstairs and change first," she said as she stood. "Give me a few minutes."

Ryan nodded and watched her go.

****

When he heard the bedroom door close, Ryan pulled out his phone and tried calling Sean again. It had been several hours since he tried and he was hoping the call would go through.

Unfortunately, it didn't.

He had a few other numbers to try – both in the U.S. and the Philippines – but he still didn't get to speak to anyone. Looking up, he saw Tricia walking down the stairs in a pair of cropped yoga pants and an oversized t-shirt. Her long hair was pulled back in a ponytail and she'd taken off all her makeup.

And yet she still looked pretty.

"Okay, my turn," he said and quickly made his way up the stairs to change. He didn't have much with him – being away from home for another night wasn't something he had planned on – but he did have a pair of sweats and a t-shirt. On a whim, he walked over to the closet and opened it. "Son of a..." he said with a laugh. The closet was still full of Sean's clothes. It was as if his brother still lived there.

And that he'd be home soon.

Well damn.

He shut the door with a little more force than was needed and cursed. Positive. He needed to stay positive. Wasn't he just telling Tricia that?

Suddenly the walls seemed to be closing in on him and Ryan quickly changed and made his escape, practically running back down the stairs. He found Tricia in the den flipping through the channels. It was a smaller room than the living room and it was dominated by a massive couch.

"Ah," he said as he sat down in one of the large corners, "TV and the big couch. Good idea."

Tricia chuckled at him. "And the big TV too."

He looked closer at the television and grinned. "Damn. When did you get this?"

"About a year ago. The one your mom left for me was ancient and wasn't very reliable with keeping a picture. When it finally went, I decided to splurge." She waved a hand in the direction of the sixty-inch flat-screen. "Best purchase I ever made."

"A woman after my own heart," he teased and immediately noticed how Tricia's smile faded and she went back to looking at the channel guide. "Okay," he said after a minute, "what have we got?"

They'd never done this before so Ryan had no idea what kind of movies Tricia preferred. In his experience, women tended to go more for the romantic comedies or dramas. That totally wasn't his thing but with it getting late and the fact that he really needed a distraction, he'd pretty much agree to anything.

"We have all the usual suspects you can find on cable just about every day of the year, but I've also got on-demand so we have more of an option. Any requests?"

Now what? Trying to be fair, Ryan suggested several different movies as Tricia scanned through their list of options. They bantered back and forth for a few minutes on the pros and cons of several titles before settling on an old cop comedy from the eighties.

The lighting in the room was dim and Ryan was stretched out at one end of the sofa while Tricia was at the other. This one piece of furniture took up nearly the entire room but right now, he remembered exactly why his mom had purchased it – because it was extremely comfortable.

The opening credits were going when Tricia turned to him. "Do you want anything to drink?"

He shook his head. "I'm good. Relax. You don't have to wait on me."

She stretched out and got more comfortable – almost lying down. "I know. I can't help it. You're a guest here…"

"Not really," he chuckled, but kept his eyes on the TV.

The movie started and that was the end of the conversation for the time being.

****

The sound of a phone ringing woke Tricia up. Lifting her head, she looked around the room and realized she was still in the den. It was a different movie playing on the television and Ryan was asleep on the other side of the couch.

The ringtone wasn't from her phone so naturally she knew it had to be his. "Ryan," she called out hoarsely. Clearing her throat, she tried again. He lifted his head and looked around dazedly. "Your phone's ringing."

He immediately jumped up and sprinted from the room to get it. He came back in a minute later. "Yes, I can hear you," he said as he came around and sat close to Tricia. "Uh-huh…okay…when?" He nodded and listened before pulling the phone away from his ear and hitting the button to put it on speaker.

"Ryan…?" she asked and he held up a finger to stop her.

The phone was quiet at first but then there was a bit of static. "Ryan? Are you there?"

Sean!

Tears were in Ryan's eyes as he looked over at Tricia and smiled. "I'm here, bro. How are you doing?"

More static. "I've been better. I can tell you that," Sean said with a slight chuckle.

"What happened? Where are you?"

"I'm at a hospital in Manila right now but they're going to fly me out of here to Hong Kong in a little bit."

"Sean," Tricia interrupted, "what happened? Are you hurt?"

"Trish?" he asked with surprise. "What are you doing with Ryan?"

"When we heard the news about the storm and that you were missing, I came to tell her in person," Ryan replied.

"Well damn," Sean said. "I wasn't really missing. I mean, the storm pretty much knocked out most lines of communications but I can't believe you guys thought…"

"The company you're subbing for called us with the news, Sean," Ryan said. "They called mom – I think his name was Dave - and then she called me and I came to Tricia's…"

"Wow. I hate that you guys got all upset over nothing."

"Um…clearly it's not nothing if you're being airlifted from one hospital to another," Tricia said. "What's going on, Sean?"

"We were in the process of moving out of the area before the storm hit. No one expected it to be quite so bad. I should have left when they first warned us." Sean paused. "But I was stubborn and wanted to get our things packed up."

"Why wouldn't you leave?" Ryan snapped. "Dammit, Sean, you need to listen to other people once in a while!"

"Yeah, okay. Spare me the lecture," Sean said. More static on the line. "A crane collapsed when the worst of the storm was hitting and I was too close to it. I got hit with some of the debris."

"What?" Both Ryan and Tricia cried in unison.

Sean sighed. "Let's just say it's gonna be a while before I'm…you know…mobile."

"Sean, what the hell happened exactly? Where are you hurt?" Ryan asked anxiously.

"My whole left side. A stack of two-by-fours came down on me. Broke my arm in two different places, my leg in three different places and some ribs. Luckily I had my hardhat on or I'd really be in bad shape, huh?" he said with a nervous chuckle.

"Not funny, bro," Ryan said. "Okay, so what do we need to do? What hospital? I can get on a plane and…"

"No," Sean said firmly. "Everything is pretty chaotic here and I'm not even sure where exactly I'm going. I'll have Dave keep you up-to-date just in case I can't get through. They're handling everything and…"

More static and then the line went dead.

"Sean?" Ryan called out, hoping they hadn't truly lost the connection. "Sean!" Reluctantly, he hung up and looked over at Tricia. "I'm going to try to get him back on the line."

All she could do was nod.

For thirty minutes, Ryan kept trying to redial and get through. He even called the few contacts he'd already made regarding Sean and couldn't get through to any of them either. Tricia got up to get them each something to drink and saw it was after three in the morning.

"Ry? Anyone here in the states isn't going to answer the phone at this hour. We need to wait until a little later in the morning and try again…maybe get some sleep."

He stood and took the glass of juice from her hands. "I can't possibly sleep. I need to find out where exactly he's going to and get there."

She shook her head. "If anything, you should be able to sleep a little easier because we talked to him and we know – for the most part – that he's all right." Taking his phone from his hand, she placed it on the coffee table. "He's alive, Ryan," she said softly and then let out a bubble of laughter. "He's alive!"

And then she essentially wrapped herself around him in an embrace as she laughed. Ryan stooped down a little and placed his juice glass on the table next to his phone before straightening and returning the hug. They stayed locked like that for several long minutes before Tricia pulled back.

Ryan's cheek was wet and Tricia realized she had actually been crying through her laughter and relief. He nodded and smiled. "He's alive." His voice was a little shaky and he reached for her again and pulled her into another embrace. "He sounded good, too, right?"

Tricia nodded. "He did. He really did." She sighed and relaxed against him. "Should we call Steph?"

This time Ryan was the one to pull back but he took one of her hands in his and gently tugged until they both sat back down on the couch. "Not now. It's too early. She's probably asleep. I'd hate to be the reason she can't fall back to sleep."

"You really won't sleep now?"

He shook his head. "My mind is racing in a million different directions." Her hand was still snuggly secured in his as he spoke. "I can't even begin to tell you how relieved I am. The thought of something like this happening to Sean? It kills me. I hate how he's over there by himself."

"Me too," she said softly, resting her head on his shoulder. "But he's right. It's probably very chaotic over there and you know he's not the only one who was hurt in the storm. We'd really just be in the way. Hopefully once they get him safely out of the country and over to Hong Kong, it won't take long until they send him home."

"Where is that anymore? He gave up his place and put all his things in storage when he left two years ago. Steph is constantly on the move and..."

"He can stay here," she said simply. "He won't be able to sleep up in his room but he can use the guest room for as long as he needs."

Ryan went silent for several minutes. "That's putting a lot of pressure on you. You have a full-time job and a life, Tricia. From what he's talking about with his injuries, he'll need constant care."

She shrugged. "Then maybe they'll fly him home to a rehab facility until he can get around a little bit more and then he can come here."

"Or he can come and stay with me. I mean...I have the space and..."

"That would be very nice, too. I'm sure Sean would like that. I didn't mean to step on your toes."

He chuckled softly. "You weren't. You're just more compassionate than I am. As relieved as I am that he's alive, part of me still wants to strangle him. If he had listened to the warnings, he wouldn't be hurt right now."

"I'm sure he's learned his lesson, Ryan. We can't harp on it. He's got enough to deal with." And then she sighed.

"What? What's the matter?"

"It's…it's nothing. Really. It's stupid."

"No. Come on. Tell me," he nudged.

"I'm a completely horrible person."

Ryan looked at her as if she was crazy. "What in the world are you talking about?"

Tears filled her eyes again. "I hate he's hurt and that he's got a long recovery ahead of him and all I can think of is how I'm going to miss out on the time we had planned to spend together!"

"You mean the weddings?"

She nodded and began to cry. "See? I'm a horrible person!"

He couldn't help but chuckle again as he put an arm around her and tucked her in close beside him. "You are the least horrible person I know, Tricia." She shook her head against him. "It's true. How many people do you know would take care of someone's family home and leave everything intact for them? I'll tell you…none. You're willing to let Sean come here to recuperate even though you know it's going to be rough. See? Not horrible. Sweet. And kind." He placed a kiss on the top of her head.

Beside him, Tricia wiped her eyes. "He's my best friend, Ryan. He's always looked out for me. How could I not do the same for him?"

"You're a good person, Tricia. I know you're disappointed about the weddings, but it can't be helped."

She yawned. "I know. He got me all excited about going with him and now...?" She yawned again and shifted beside him.

"It will all be okay," he said softly, sitting back and relaxing a little more against the cushions. Tricia moved with him, her head still on his shoulder. "I promise."

Her only response was a soft snore.

Four

Two weeks later Ryan was pulling back up to Tricia's house. He parked in the driveway and sighed. The last time he was here had been to give her the news about Sean. Well, he'd been in contact with his brother every day since he left here and now he was essentially back for the same reason.

News about Sean.

Wasn't this what phones were invented for?

With a bit of a growl, he climbed from the car and walked to the front door. Her car was in the driveway so he didn't feel right about using his key and letting himself in. So he rang the bell and waited. Shifting uncomfortably, he wondered if he should have called first.

"Ryan!" Tricia said as she opened the door. "What a surprise!" She motioned for him to come in. "Were you working out this way again?"

"Uh…no," he said, raking a hand through his hair. "Listen, is this…is this a good time? I wanted to talk to you about something."

She was walking toward the kitchen – no doubt to offer him something to drink. He followed and accepted the soda she handed him. "So what's going on? Is everything okay? I talked to Sean yesterday and he seems to be getting stronger every day."

Ryan nodded and looked around the kitchen. "Can we maybe go and sit down?"

"O-kay," she said slowly, following him out to the living room and taking a seat on the sofa next to him. "You're starting to freak me out, Ryan. What's up?"

Instead of answering right away, he finished his soda and put the glass down on the coffee table. Then he pulled out his phone and scrolled through a couple of screens. When he found what he was looking for, he turned to face her.

"Sean sent me this message this morning," he said solemnly. Then he held the phone out for her to be able to see the screen.

"Is it a video?"

He nodded and hit play.

"Hey, bro! How's life in the states? I seriously cannot wait to get home and have these casts off and maybe have some pizza and beers with you. I can probably still do that here but it's not quite the same," he chuckled. "Okay, so I have to do this quick – I'm not sure how long these video things last and the nurse is holding the camera for me. So…here's the thing. I'm not going to make it home any time soon. I'm going to be here at least another four weeks and then I'll be flying home for rehab. I promised Trish we'd go to these weddings together."

He paused and then chuckled again. "Actually, I kind of made her promise to go with me. Last summer we went to a couple of weddings – stag – and they were nightmares. I don't want her to have to deal with that again. It's my fault she's being forced to go alone and I hate it for her."

The camera seemed to falter and shake and then righted again. "If you're watching this, Tricia, I'm really sorry. You know I wanted us to go to these together. I totally screwed that up, huh?" He smiled bashfully. "Leave it to me to take something simple and make it complicated." Another pause. "So here's the thing, I want the two of you to go to the weddings together. Ryan, I want you to go in my place. Please. I know you hate weddings but I think if the two of you go together, you'll actually have a lot of fun. Stick to the original plan – pretend to be a couple and just have a good time."

Tricia looked nervously over at Ryan before looking back at the screen. "I love you guys – other than mom, there's no one else I care about more. So…do this. For me. We've already RSVP'd to all of them so I know you're still gonna go, Trish. Just…don't go alone. Don't put yourself in that position. And Ry? I know you've bailed my ass out of a lot of things in my life and I swear at some point I'll make it up to you, but if you could do it one more time, I'd really appreciate it." He yawned and seemed to grimace with a bit of pain. "Just think about it, okay? For me?"

And then the video ended.

They sat in silence and Ryan had to wonder what she was thinking. He'd had a couple of hours to wrap his brain around the message but for Tricia, this was brand-new information.

On the surface, it didn't seem like a big deal.

Go to some weddings. Eat, drink and be merry.

But for some reason, Ryan had a feeling there was more to it and he wasn't sure how to proceed.

Of course he'd do this for his brother. Hell, it was the least he could do. The thing that was really eating at him more than anything was how he never seemed sure of what the true nature of Sean and Tricia's relationship was.

Were they really just friends?

Did his brother have a thing for Tricia?

Years ago Ryan had said something to Sean about it and Sean had vehemently denied feeling anything more than friendship for Tricia. Ryan had never quite believed it and for some reason, it made this whole situation seem even more awkward.

He cleared his throat. "So…um…what do you think?"

Tricia was staring at her hands, and he didn't take that as a good sign.

"Trish?"

When she finally looked up, she wouldn't quite meet his gaze. "I…I don't know. I mean, I don't want you to feel obligated. I already knew Sean wasn't going to be able to go and I'm okay with it."

"Oh." Why did it bother him so much? She was essentially giving him a free pass. So why didn't he just take it and run?

"It wasn't fair of Sean to ask that of you," she went on. "I mean, I was looking forward to going – with him – but I'll be fine. Really. It will be fine."

Maybe if she didn't keep saying "fine" he would have believed her. Or maybe it was the way she seemed to be rambling more to herself than to him. Either way, Ryan knew what he was going to do.

Shaking his head, he reached over and patted the back of her hand. "No can do, Trish. I'm not going to let my brother down on this one. You're stuck with me."

****

Okay, it was one thing to go to the weddings with Sean and pretend to be lovers; it was quite another to go with his brother. Sean was her best friend and she felt comfortable with him. But Ryan? Well, she was really just getting to know him. That's not to say she didn't *know* him but lately she was really getting to learn about the kind of man he was.

And she was starting to like it.

A lot.

Maybe a little too much.

He was looking at her expectantly and for the life of her, Tricia had no idea what to do or say. He wasn't Sean. And that wasn't a bad thing, per se, but she just wasn't sure how she was supposed to be around him.

And throwing in the fake relationship thing certainly wasn't helping matters.

"I really don't think it's necessary, Ryan. Besides, it would be awkward."

"Why?"

Her eyes widened at the question. Was he for real? How could it be anything but? "Look, the thing is…you're not Sean. Sean and I have known one another for years and we're…well, I think we're closer to one another than we are to anyone else." She met his eyes. "No offense."

Ryan shook his head and smiled. "None taken."

"We just have a connection and even with that, I wasn't sure if we could pull anything off." She shrugged. "I just don't think you and I can go out there and pretend anything that people would believe."

He studied her for a minute. "Okay, how about this – we just go together, as friends. I'll be going to represent Sean and I'll be there by your side so no one can throw any shade at you. What do you think?"

What did she think? It sounded like a plausible plan, but did she really want to go with Ryan to all of those events? "You know it's six weddings right? Like all summer long this is going to go on."

He shrugged. "Summer is three months long and you're telling me six days out of the entire summer, I'll have to dress up and socialize. I think I can handle it."

"You'll essentially be giving up your weekends," she quickly added. "I mean, you live in Jersey, all the weddings are here so...you know. You'll need to come in Friday night for a Saturday wedding and then stay over and go home Sunday. It's a lot of time away from home. I'm sure you have things you like to do on the weekends."

"Not really," he said, his smile widening.

"Oh." She was beginning to feel a bit dejected. Life would be a lot easier if he would just take the out she was handing him and run with it, but no. He had to be admirable and want to help his brother.

At any other time it would be an attractive quality in a man.

But not right now.

With a loud sigh, Tricia stood up. "I'm not talking you out of this, am I?"

Ryan shook his head. "I think it could be fun," he said, still grinning.

"You're a lousy liar just like Sean," she said as she picked up their glasses and walked to the kitchen. "If I had been smarter, I would have called everyone right after Sean's accident and just backed out of all the damn weddings."

"You wouldn't do that," he said from right behind her. For a minute he simply stood and watched her rinse the glasses and put them in the dishwasher. "You know you really want to go to these weddings and I think part of you is relieved to have someone going with you. Now I realize I'm not my brother, but I'm not trying to be. We can be as casual about why we're there together or as outlandish as you want. I'm just going to follow your lead."

Great. And he was going to be a gentleman too.

Slamming the dishwasher door with a little more force than necessary, she faced Ryan, her arms crossed over her chest. "Fine."

He mimicked her pose. "Fine? That's all you have to say is fine?"

"What am I supposed to say?" She could feel her lips twitching with the need to smile at his imitation of her.

"How about 'Gee, Ryan, thanks. I bet we'll have a great time.' Or maybe 'Thanks, Ryan. I don't know how I would have dealt with all these weddings without you.'"

Each phrase was said in a voice that Tricia guessed was supposed to sound like her and that did have her smiling. So doing her best, she imitated that voice right back to him, repeating those phrases. They were both laughing hard by the time she was done.

"That's better," he finally said and turned toward the wall board with all the invitations on them. Clapping his hands together, he rubbed them before going back to the living room to get his phone. "Okay, now let's get all these dates down on my calendar so I know where I'm supposed to be and when."

For the next thirty minutes, Tricia dictated the dates and whose weddings they were attending and when. She felt the need to give a little background information with each couple, and by the time they were done, Ryan's eyes were a little glazed over.

"You know I'm not going to remember any of that, right?"

She nodded. "I know but it just seemed like the thing to do."

"So this first one is on a Friday night," he said, scrolling back over the calendar. "Would it be all right for me to get here that afternoon – maybe after lunch?"

"That should be fine. I won't be here, but you can let yourself in and get yourself ready."

"Where are you going to be? Work?"

She shook her head. "No, I took the day off so I could do all of the girlie things that need to be done before going to a wedding."

"Girlie things? What exactly does that even mean?"

"Oh…um…I'm going to get my hair done, manicure, pedicure…you know, the basics." She looked at her own calendar to make sure she didn't miss anything. "Besides, I have to make sure I look good for my boyfriend." She almost couldn't saying it without smirking.

"Damn right you do," he agreed, chuckling. "While you're at it, make sure you wear something slinky, okay?"

She gave him a look that let him know exactly what she thought of him at that moment and swatted him with an invitation.

"Hey! All I'm saying is that I have a reputation to maintain."

Tricia burst out laughing. "Now you sound exactly like your brother!"

"Well, just make sure you don't laugh at all the things I say when we're around other people. They'll get suspicious if every time I say something boyfriend-ish or touch you, you start to laugh."

She hadn't thought about that. "I don't think it will be a problem. I still don't think we'll have to do a whole lot of anything. Just the fact that I have a date with me should be enough to keep the pity-partiers at bay."

He stood and stretched. "Well, if not, I'm here."

She wasn't sure yet if it was a good thing or a bad one.

****

Tricia had invited Ryan to stay the night since it was a three-hour drive back to his place in Jersey. He had readily accepted and they had decided to go out to dinner again. He was back in his old room relaxing while she had gone to take a shower.

As she stood under the steaming hot spray, she was deep in thought. In all the years she'd known the Petersons, she'd never spent this much time with Ryan. It was awkward and…comfortable all at the same time.

Hell, who was she kidding? It was more comfortable than awkward.

Ryan Peterson had been a good-looking teenager and he was now a devastatingly handsome man, the kind who looked good without even trying. And he wasn't her best friend. And he wasn't off limits. She let out a sigh and turned off the water. *Where the hell did that thought even come from?* She thought.

As she was toweling off, she heard Ryan moving around in his room. Quickly, she went through her routine of putting on her moisturizer and brushing her teeth. When she was done, she realized she hadn't brought a robe into the bathroom with her. She wasn't used to having someone else in the house and normally walking back to her room in just a towel wouldn't be a big deal. Feeling confident that Ryan was doing his own thing, she opened the door and stepped out into the hallway.

Just as Ryan was stepping out into the hallway himself.

"Oh!" she cried as they nearly collided. She tried not to meet his eyes.

"Sorry," he mumbled as he kept his gaze averted and moved around her. "I was just heading downstairs to wait until you were ready."

"Um…no big deal," she said nervously as she headed toward her bedroom. *Awkward. Awkward. Awkward.* In the doorway, she turned and then their eyes did meet – briefly – before she closed the door. And then she stood there with her back against the bedroom door for several long moments until her racing heart calmed down.

Ryan, on the other hand, stood rooted to the spot long after the door had closed. As he had watched her walk past, he had taken note of her trim figure and the long expanse of silky legs. There had been small moisture droplets all over her and for the briefest of moments, he tried to imagine how they felt sliding down her smooth skin.

He knew he shouldn't be thinking of Tricia like that and then stopped himself. Why not? Why shouldn't he think of her like that, as an attractive woman? It's what she was! She wasn't his best friend and although there was still a little gray area on how exactly Sean felt about her, Ryan knew he basically had nothing to feel bad about.

But maybe he should call Sean and clear some things up first.

Looking at his watch, he did the time difference math and then rationalized that Tricia would probably be upstairs getting ready for at least a few more minutes and knew he'd have plenty of time to talk to his brother.

Stepping out onto the back deck, he made the call. "Hey, bro," he said when Sean answered. "How are you feeling?"

"Good," he said. "Really good. If it weren't for this body cast, I'd be fantastic."

Ryan couldn't help but laugh. Sean always had a way of making light of things.

"So I take it you got my video message."

"Yeah, I did. And as a matter of fact, I'm here at Tricia's now."

"And? You're gonna do it, right? You're going to go with her to all these weddings so she doesn't have to go alone, right?"

"Yeah, yeah. Of course," Ryan said quickly. "But...can I just ask you something?"

"Sure. What's up?"

"Why? Why is this so important to you? I mean, people would understand why you're not there with her. Why not just let it go? It's not like you don't have other things to be focusing on. Which reminds me, any word on when you're coming home?"

"One topic at a time, Ry. It's still early here," Sean chuckled. "First, no. I don't have a date on when I'm coming home. It's only been two weeks and it's too soon to see how things are healing. If I had to guess, I'd say I'm going to be here for at least another month."

"Are you sure you're okay? Mom's chomping at the bit to fly over there and be with you and I can't blame her. I'd be sitting right next to her on that flight."

"We've been over this already and I thought you both understood. There's nothing you can do here. I'm going to need you both more when I get home. I'll call mom tonight and put her mind at ease. And as for you, you can't get away. Your summer is going to be pretty full now that you're taking my place at all those weddings."

"Which brings me back to my original question – why is this such a big deal to you? Tricia didn't seem all that bothered with going on her own. So if she's okay with it, why aren't you?"

There was a lot of static on the line again and Ryan cursed. "Sean? Sean? Are you there?"

The static broke up a little. "…so you can see why it's important to me," Sean said when the line cleared.

"What? No. No! I didn't hear what you said!" he growled with frustration. "Look, I'm going to do this. I'm going with her, I just…I need to know what the deal is."

"I just told you…"

"And I told you the static made it impossible for me to hear. C'mon, man. Just say it again."

"I love her."

"You…you're in love with Tricia?" The news hit Ryan like a sucker punch. It was one thing to think it; it was another to have it confirmed. *Shit.*

"Well…yeah. I thought you knew," Sean said casually.

"I…I guess I knew you guys were really close but…love? Are…are you sure? Is that why you came up with this crazy plan to go to these things as a couple? Were you hoping that playing make-believe would turn into the real thing?"

"Wait, wait, wait…what are you talking about?"

"You!" Ryan snapped. "You just said you're in love with Tricia!"

"What? No!" Sean laughed. "I mean, yes, I love her, but no, I'm not in love with her. Sorry, our connection isn't the greatest."

Relief washed over Ryan with more force than it should have. He sat down on one of the teak benches by the pond and let out a shaky sigh. His brother wasn't in love with Tricia. The coast was clear.

An image of Tricia wrapped in her towel came to mind and Ryan let it stay there for a minute.

"Ry?"

"What? Oh…um…yeah. Okay. I guess I just thought maybe you had an ulterior motive for wanting to play pretend couple with her."

"Dude, she's like a sister to me and I hate to see her get her feelings hurt. People don't always realize they're being mean and…well…I know it bothers Trish that she's not in a relationship right now. It was actually a win-win situation for us both. We had each other's backs. And if I can't be there to look out for her, I feel better knowing you are. I trust you. So…thanks. "

Well that put a whole different spin on the situation.

And not really a good one.

Sean was trusting him to look after Tricia and make sure no one hurt her or hurt her feelings. Ryan knew he was growing more and more attracted to her the more time they spent together, but that didn't mean he was looking for something long-term or permanent. And he'd hate to be the guy who hurt her and then have to deal with his brother when he got back to the states and found out.

That only left one solution – take a step back and go back to looking at Tricia like he used to. She was his younger brother's friend. Nothing more, nothing less.

The image of her in the towel made another appearance.

It was going to be one hell of a long summer.

Five

"That was a great party," Tricia stated as she sank comfortably into the passenger seat of Ryan's BMW. They had just left their first wedding reception and she was feeling extremely happy and carefree. "I think we pulled it off."

Ryan had to agree. When he'd shown up at Tricia's earlier that day, she hadn't been home, as she had warned him. The entire drive there he had agonized over how the night was going to go and how he was supposed to play this role of wedding date. They hadn't discussed specifics and instead had decided to go with the flow.

The flow, it turned out, was that they were a new couple. Tricia – without any warning – had started telling people they'd only been dating a couple of weeks, since Sean's accident. It wasn't a complete lie, he supposed. Other than the dating part. But they had started spending time together since they'd gotten news about his brother.

Everyone had been really friendly and he spent half the night giving people updates on his brother and the other half laughing and dancing with Tricia.

And damn if it didn't feel good.

He realized she was looking at him. "I'm sorry. What?" he asked distractedly.

"I said I think we pulled it off. What do you think?" Her eyes were drooping and her voice was soft and just a little bit sleepy.

It was sexy as hell.

"Absolutely," he said, forcing his focus back on the road because it would be very easy to keep looking at her. "You were an excellent date."

"Why thank you," she said with a smile, her eyes closing. "It was so good to see everyone again! I know you really didn't know any of them, but Sean and I have been friends with them for as long as I can remember. He introduced me to most of them the first week I moved here and we've never lost touch."

"That's a good thing. It doesn't always happen," Ryan said, thinking of his own friends he'd lost contact with over the years.

"I had forgotten how much fun we all used to have. I didn't realize how much I've missed them all. I mean, we talk on the phone and keep up with each other on Facebook, but it's been a while since we all just hung out. And now we'll get to see most of them again Sunday at wedding number two."

"That one is in the early afternoon, right?"

Tricia nodded. "Mm-hmm."

"I plan on driving back to Jersey after I bring you home if that's all right with you. I've got work on Monday, so…"

She reached across the car and touched his hand. "Ryan, you don't need to ask my permission." She smiled. "You're the one doing me a favor by going to the wedding with me. It's completely okay for you to go home when you want to."

Yeah, he knew that, but for some reason the thought of just dropping her off wasn't appealing.

Tonight had been a good night. No, a great one. Ryan couldn't remember the last time he'd enjoyed himself so much. It wasn't that he cared one way or the other about the wedding itself, but being with Tricia had been...good. He was finding they had a lot more in common than he ever realized and she had a great sense of humor and when they danced she felt amazing in his arms.

Lines were getting blurred and right now Ryan didn't have the will to care.

They pulled up in front of the house and Ryan walked around to the passenger side of the car to help Tricia out. When she placed her hand in his, he felt that buzz of attraction he'd been feeling all night every time they touched. Did she feel it too?

Tricia trembled slightly as she came to her feet.

"Cold?" he asked, his voice low and gravelly.

Her eyes were wide for a moment and then her features relaxed as she shook her head. "I'm good," she said. "Just looking forward to getting inside and kicking these shoes off."

Looking down, Ryan admired the stilettos. They'd been making him crazy all night. In combination with the jade green strapless dress she was wearing, the look was lethal.

Together they walked to the door and into the house. Tricia immediately kicked the shoes off and sighed, wiggling her toes. "Sweet relief."

Yeah, she was killing him.

Turning, she walked to the kitchen and I was surprised to see her open the freezer. He followed. "What are you doing?" And then he saw the ice cream carton and laughed. "Seriously? At this hour?"

Without hesitation, Tricia walked over, grabbed a spoon and dug into the chocolate ice cream. "I told you. It's my weakness."

"But we had dessert," he reminded as he walked toward her, loosening his tie and still chuckling.

"Not the same," she countered. "Cake is one thing, but ice cream is completely different." Then she relaxed against the cabinets. "So good."

Ryan knew he was going to need a cold shower or…

He opened the freezer and grabbed the carton of chocolate chip, a spoon and a seat at the breakfast nook. Tricia watched him and smiled.

"Okay, I can see where you're coming from," he said and together they happily ate their late-night snack.

When they were done, Tricia slowly made her way to the stairs. Ryan wasn't far behind her. She made it up only one step before she turned. This almost had them at eye level. "I had a really good time with you tonight."

He nodded. "Me too."

The house was mostly dark around them. Slowly, Tricia leaned forward and placed a kiss on Ryan's cheek. Her lips lingered for just the briefest of seconds but it was enough that Ryan noticed. "Thank you," she said softly.

Unable to resist, he reached up and cupped her cheek in his hand. His thumb stroking her soft skin. Then he leaned in and gently claimed her lips with his. It was short and it was sweet and when he lifted his head he had a feeling things would never be the same again.

Slowly Tricia's eyes opened and when she looked at him, Ryan knew he was right. It was already different. There was a kaleidoscope of emotion playing there. He stroked her cheek one more time before wishing her a good night.

Then, taking a step back, he watched her go up the stairs and didn't move until he heard her bedroom door close.

****

Saturday morning dawned bright and sunny. Tricia slept late and figured Ryan would do the same. Actually, she hoped he'd at least sleep later than her so she had more time to come to grips with the kiss they'd shared last night.

It wasn't that it was passionate or that they'd gotten out of control, but it had seriously been more potent than any kiss she'd ever experienced. It had taken every ounce of self-control she had to walk up the stairs and away from him. What she really wanted was to lean back in for another kiss. And then another until they were both breathless.

Yeah, self-control sucked.

Forcing herself to rise from the bed, she threw on a pair of shorts and a t-shirt, pulled her hair up into a ponytail and opened the bedroom door. Ryan's door was open so she could only assume he was already awake. She found him down in the kitchen reading the paper and drinking coffee at the breakfast nook.

Her tummy fluttered nervously and she wondered how she was supposed to act now. Did she kiss him good morning? Or keep it casual?

"Hey, how'd you sleep?" he asked pleasantly when she walked into the room.

"Oh...um...fine, thanks. And you?"

"Great. It amazes me how I can sleep that well in a twin bed. It's hard to believe I used to sleep in that thing growing up. Back home I've got a king size bed and yet I didn't feel the need to stretch out as much last night. I fell asleep as soon as my head hit the pillow."

She really wished he'd stop talking about beds and pillows and stretching out all over them. With a small smile, she made her way over to the coffee maker and poured herself a cup. "That's good."

Folding the paper, Ryan looked at her as if everything was completely the same and that's when she knew she was the only one affected by the kiss. Well, darn. It definitely sucked but she'd get over it. At least she knew where she stood now. That was a good thing, right?

Yeah, keep telling yourself that.

"I was thinking about having lunch out on the deck," Ryan said after a minute. "It's after eleven and if you'd like, I can go to the deli and grab us some sandwiches. What do you think?"

"I've got the makings here. You don't have to go anyplace."

He stood and stretched. "Nah. Not the same."

Tricia trailed after him as he walked out of the room and toward the front door. "It's really not a big deal, Ryan. I don't mind making us some lunch."

He turned and gave her a patient smile. "Let me ask you this – do you have any Italian bread?"

"No, but I do have…"

"Do you have any bacon?"

She shook her head.

"Roast beef? Provolone? Barbecue potato chips? Potato salad? Pickles?"

"Okay, no I don't have any of those things but what I have is just as good!"

"Okay, lay it on me. What have you got?"

She walked back to the kitchen and pulled the refrigerator door open. "I've got turkey breast, Swiss cheese, some tuna fish and some whole wheat sandwich thins." Peeking out from behind the door, she grinned sheepishly. "Yeah, okay. Go to the deli."

Quickly she rambled off her sandwich order and watched him leave. While he was gone she set up the table on the deck and got out everything they'd need and then sat herself down on one of the chaise lounges to get some sun.

It was a beautiful day with just the right combination of heat and cool breezes and she was content to simply stay where she was. With a sigh of contentment, she closed her eyes. This was good. Ryan didn't seem to be fazed by the kiss, so things could go on as normal. It was for the best. Maybe later they'd call Sean together and talk to him. Other than that, she had no real plans for the day. She didn't think they had to spend the whole day together and if Ryan had something he wanted to do, she certainly wouldn't stop him.

The image of them on the stairs last night came to her mind. Okay, maybe Ryan wasn't fazed by the damn kiss, but she still was. Kind of. Okay, a lot. If he had the ability to make her feel weak and needy with barely the touch of his lips, what would he be like if it was a full-on experience?

And as she squirmed on the chaise, Tricia realized how much she really wanted to know.

It didn't matter that he was Sean's brother.

It didn't matter that it could make things all kinds of awkward if they were to get involved.

There were five more weddings for them to get through. How was she supposed to play the part of his girlfriend when being close to Ryan was now going to mess with her senses?

Now she wanted to know how he really kissed. And how his hands would feel roaming over her. Or how the scratchy skin of his jaw would feel. Or what it would feel like if she bit him...

She groaned.

And tried to think of a dozen different things she could do to keep distance between them for the rest of the day.

****

They were sitting in church the next day and Ryan felt a little ill at ease.

Tricia had pretty much kept her distance yesterday after lunch and he had a feeling it was because he'd kissed her. Dammit. It had been a stupid impulse and he hadn't meant to make things awkward between them. It was probably a good thing this was an early afternoon wedding and he'd be gone and on the road by six. Then they'd have a week before they had to see one another again.

If she wanted to even see him again.

They were sitting in a pew and Tricia was talking to several friends in the row behind them when Ryan saw her sort of freeze and go pale. He was about to ask if she was all right when he noticed a few other heads looking in the same direction as she was.

"I didn't think he'd come," several of them were saying and if Ryan had to guess, he'd say that the guy who'd just walked into the church had to be an ex-boyfriend of Tricia's. *Shit.* He had no idea about who she'd dated or what kind of situations were involved and with the time difference, there was no way for him to text Sean to find out.

He leaned in close and murmured, "Are you okay?"

She nodded but didn't look at him.

Not a good sign.

The only thing Ryan could do is reach for her hand and hold onto it. It took her a minute but she did eventually turn and give him a weak smile. Before he could question her, the music started and everyone stood.

By the time the ceremony was over, Tricia seemed a little more relaxed and he decided to simply let the matter go for now. If she seemed overly anxious to leave the church, he didn't question it. And when she decided they should go on ahead of everyone to the reception hall, he didn't say a word.

It wasn't until they were seated with eight of her friends at the reception that he saw her tense up again. People were up and dancing and he decided she needed a distraction. Standing, he held out a hand to her. "Would you like to dance?"

Her smile was full of gratitude as she stood and let him lead her onto the dance floor. They swayed to the ballad and Ryan felt the instant she let herself relax. "Better?" he asked.

"Much." She rested her head on his shoulder.

"Care to tell me who's behind all this tension?"

And then she tensed up, looking at him with unease.

"Come on," he coaxed. "You've been tense and distant ever since the church."

She sighed. "Steve's here."

"Okay," he said slowly. "And who's Steve?"

"My ex. We dated for four years. Last two years of high school and then after." She shook her head. "I'm a little annoyed that no one gave me the heads up he was going to be here."

"So I take it the breakup was bad."

"Is there really such a thing as a good one?" she asked with a hint of sarcasm. Then she shrugged. "I don't know. To me, it was bad. He lied, he cheated and…it was pretty awful. Sean can't stand him either. Even back in high school he used to beg me to break up with him, but I wouldn't listen. Guess I should have."

"It wasn't his call to make," Ryan said simply. "Sometimes we need to go through things for ourselves." He looked around the room. "So I guess you'd like to just avoid this guy, right?"

She nodded.

"Well, at least we know he's not seated at our table. That's a good thing." He continued to look around. "Have you seen or spoken to him since you two broke up?"

She shook her head. "He called a lot in the beginning but I never took his calls. Now I get an occasional voicemail or text from him."

Ryan looked at her like she was crazy. "Why? What could he possibly have to say?"

"Oh…you know, the usual. Wanting to say hi. Just making sure I was doing okay. He was thinking of me. Blah, blah, blah. It doesn't matter. I never respond."

"I don't blame you." They went back to companionable silence and listened to the music. Another ballad started and Ryan was thankful for it. He felt himself relaxing a bit when…

"Mind if I cut in?" Came a deep male voice. Ryan didn't turn around, but he could tell by the look on Tricia's face who had asked the question.

"You know," Ryan began as he looked over his shoulder, "I think I do." Then he pulled Tricia a little tighter and moved away. It took a few seconds before he realized Tricia was staring at him. "What?"

"Don't you think that was a little rude?"

"Seriously? Did you want to dance with him?"

"Well…no but…"

"Then don't give it another thought. Clearly this guy isn't good at taking your hints. I think I made it perfectly clear for him." When the music ended, they walked off the dance floor and back to their seats. They immediately got caught up in conversations around the table and for that Ryan was grateful.

It was after five when the wedding ended and he stood and watched Tricia say goodbye to all of her friends – until next month. He thought it was kind of funny how they were all acting as if they'd never see one another again. When she was back by his side as they walked to his car, he could see that all of her earlier tension was gone.

"Thank you," she said softly.

"For what?"

"For…understanding. You didn't push and you didn't want to make a big deal out of the whole thing and I appreciate it."

He couldn't help but shrug. "It really wasn't my place. But know this…" He stopped, put his hands on her shoulders and turned her toward him. "If he had gotten out of line, if he had said or done anything to upset you, I would not have hesitated to set him straight. Wedding or no wedding, I would have taken care of it."

Then he waited to see how she would respond. Tricia's eyes scanned his face and for a minute, he didn't think she was going to say anything. Then she gave him a slow smile. "Luckily it didn't come to that. I would hate to think the wedding would have been ruined because of me."

"Not you, sweetheart. Him."

Ryan watched her swallow hard, her eyes lightly welling with tears. He took a step closer and reached up to cup her cheek. The need to touch her was almost overwhelming. All around them, people were chatting and walking to their cars but Ryan barely noticed. All he could see was Tricia.

"Well, aren't you two cozy?" Ryan didn't have to even turn his head to know it was Steve's voice. "A little incestuous, don't you think?"

With a soft stroke of his thumb across Tricia's cheek, Ryan turned and faced Steve. "Excuse me?"

"You know…all the years she had your brother at her beck and call and now here you are." Then he looked at Tricia. "Keeping it in the family, huh?"

And just like that, Ryan saw red. Without thinking, he reached out and grabbed Steve by the lapels. He caught the man off guard and when they were practically nose to nose, he nearly growled. "Listen, I don't know what your deal is and I don't want to know. I think Tricia has more than proven she wants nothing to do with you. I don't want to hear you've called her, texted her or even spoken her name, are we clear?"

"Or what?" Steve sneered right back.

"I'm not as nice as my brother," Ryan said and shoved Steve with enough force to send him stumbling several feet away. "Of course, if you'd like to find out just how different we are, stick around a little longer."

Steve got to his feet, his face red, fists clenched at his side. He glared at Ryan and then looked over at Tricia who was standing there wringing her hands. "You know what? Forget it. You're not worth it." And he turned and walked away.

Ryan stood rooted to the spot and didn't move until he saw the guy get in his car and drive away. Then he turned back to Tricia. "You okay?"

She nodded. "I...I'm so sorry. I didn't mean for you to have to get involved. It was really stupid and childish of me. I keep saying I'm fine and over him – and I am – but when I see him or hear his voice it just...I don't know. I get so mad and freaked out that it almost paralyzes me. How stupid is that?"

He stepped in close and wrapped her in his arms, grateful when she hugged him back. "I don't think it's stupid at all. I think it's pretty normal." He tightened his arms once before letting her go, taking her hand and leading her to his car. "I'm sorry he upset you."

"Right now, I'm more upset with myself." They climbed into the car and it wasn't until they were almost home when Tricia spoke again. "I'm sure you're anxious to get home and get away from my high school drama."

Actually, he wasn't. And he wasn't sure how he felt about it.

Unaware of his internal dilemma, she continued. "I'd completely understand if you wanted to back out of the rest of the weddings. It's basically a lot of the same people so there's a good chance Steve will show up again. I'm sure he won't bother me, and now that this happened, I think my reaction will be a lot different the next time."

Ryan didn't want to think about there being a next time. The guy was a real jackass who seemed to have a bit of a mean streak. The thought of Tricia having to deal with that on her own wasn't an option.

They pulled into her driveway and when he parked and shut the car off, she looked at him quizzically. "Were you coming in? I thought you were anxious to get on the road."

And now she was trying to get rid of him? Ryan wasn't sure why it bothered him so much, but it did.

Without a word, he got out of the car and stalked to the front door, using his key to get in.

Tricia was only a few feet behind him. "Ryan? Are you okay?"

He tossed his keys on the entryway table as he loosened his tie and kept walking toward the back deck, Tricia fast on his heels. She called his name again once they were outside and Ryan simply stopped and let his head fall back.

"What's going on?" she asked softly. "I don't understand what you're so angry about."

And that was it. That was all it took to bring his frustration to the surface. "You don't understand?" he mimicked as he turned around and started walking toward her. "Seriously?"

She shook her head. "No...I don't. I mean, I know you were angry earlier because of Steve but...I thought that was over." She took several steps backwards as he kept advancing.

"Yeah, I'm upset about Steve," he said curtly. "I can't understand what you even saw in him."

"I was young and back then, he was different," she said, a slight tremor in her voice.

"I don't want you to see him at any of these other weddings. I know it's not my call to make but I can't help it. I don't want him near you, upsetting you."

That seemed to relax her a little. "Tonight was a bit eye-opening. It had been a while and I guess by not responding to him all this time, he wasn't getting the point. I'm sure he does now."

"Not good enough." They were stepping back into the house. "If there's a chance of him being at any of these other weddings, then I'm going to be there with you."

"Oh…okay," she said and then paused. "I just don't want you to be so…upset. Angry. I know I kind of overreacted earlier. I didn't mean to drag you into this mess."

"I'm not angry!" he yelled and then realized how ridiculous it sounded considering the tone of his voice. Raking a hand through his hair, he closed his eyes and mentally counted to ten.

When he had thought about this weekend, it seemed like such a short amount of time and now it seemed as if it was lasting forever. Ryan knew he should have just gotten in the car and left, but he couldn't. He was too wound up and restless and the thought of spending three hours in the car with nothing to do but think was beyond unappealing.

The entire situation was getting out of hand. It was supposed to be simple – go with Tricia to some weddings. That's it. Sure there was the whole fake relationship angle, but he hadn't counted on any real feelings coming in to play. Looking at her now, he realized just how wrong he was. Not only were there real feelings, but they were strong. Very strong.

Too strong.

Tricia was studying him hard and Ryan knew he was going to have to say something to try and explain why he was freaking out. "Look, I just didn't like seeing you so upset. Personally, I don't understand it, but that's none of my business. I'm doing Sean a favor and making sure no one upsets you and…"

To his surprise, Tricia was the one to snap. "So that's what this is all about? Like hanging out with me is some sort of chore?" She snorted with disgust and shoved past him to get out of the kitchen. In the hallway she kicked off her shoes. "I am so sick and tired of everyone thinking they know what's best for me or treating me as if I can't think for myself."

"What are you talking about?" he asked, following after her.

"It doesn't matter," she snapped, walking over to the front door and opening it. "You have a long drive ahead of you and you should go."

He looked at her incredulously. "You're throwing me out?"

She nodded. "I don't need a babysitter. I can handle myself. I'll admit I didn't realize until tonight just how out of control I'd let things get. If it were Sean here with me, I'd be giving him the same lecture. I'm a grown woman and it's time I started acting like one. I'll deal with whatever comments anyone throws my way at the rest of the weddings. They're no more insulting than needing someone to fight my battles for me. I'm not a child and like I said…no more babysitter."

He glared at her but stayed where he was. "I don't appreciate being referred to as a babysitter. I'm here because my brother..."

"Yeah, yeah, yeah...he asked you to. He asked you to watch out for me. Well...newsflash. I don't want to be looked after. If I don't have a real date to go with me, then I'd rather go alone. It's a lot less humiliating."

He sighed loudly. "Seriously, Tricia, what's this all about? I thought everything was pretty much okay. You didn't seem to mind me taking Sean's place when we talked about this."

She shrugged. "Well now I do. Sean's always looked out for me and I think we're both a little too old for that anymore. He's my best friend and I love him but..." She took a steadying breath, "I need to handle things on my own."

This time he did step closer, crowded her. "No one says you aren't handling things on your own, Tricia."

"Really? It seemed to me I didn't speak a word to Steve tonight. You did it all for me."

She had him there. "Okay, fine. I stepped in without thinking. I just reacted. That doesn't make me a bad guy."

"No but it made me realize how this is what I do – what I always do – and I don't like it." She leaned back against the door. "So thank you for helping me out this weekend, but for the remainder of the weddings, I'll be on my own."

Ryan shook his head. "I don't think so." He closed the distance between them. Tricia's eyes went wide. He reached up and touched her cheek.

"Why?" she whispered, her eyes scanning his face. "And don't you dare say it's because of Sean."

It was as if she could read his mind.

"It's not," he murmured huskily.

"Then why?" Her voice was barely audible.

"Because...this." He lowered his head and claimed her lips with his.

Six

Ryan was kissing her.

Really kissing her.

This wasn't an innocent peck on the cheek or anything like the kiss they'd shared the other night. This was all wet and deep and filled with need. Tricia's back was against the door and his hands – those gloriously rough hands – cupped her cheek.

Finally!

How was it possible that she'd known him all these years and hadn't felt such a pull of attraction to him? How had she gone this long in her life without being kissed by him? Wanted by him?

It didn't take long for things to escalate and somehow they were moving away from the door, Ryan slamming it closed before backing her up toward the den. Thank God. The thought of breaking the kiss and making it up the flight of stairs was more than she could handle right now.

Both of their hands were exploring and touching as they moved from one room to the next. Her eyes were closed and she felt almost too lazy to open them; besides, it made everything that was happening a total sensory experience. Taking away her ability to really see Ryan but being able to touch and feel him? It was quite exciting.

He whispered her name as his lips left hers at the same time her legs hit the back of the massive couch. Her head fell back, her long hair spilling behind her as he nipped, licked and kissed the slender column of her throat. When he whispered it again, it was a plea and Tricia could only sigh and say "yes."

The next thing she knew, they were on the sofa. She kicked her shoes off as Ryan settled beside her – his hands roaming all over her from calf to shoulder – but never stopping for long. Mentally she was begging him to stop and pay attention to some of the good parts, but when his lips came back to hers, she couldn't think at all.

Her hand anchored in his hair as he slanted his lips over hers again and again until she felt like she couldn't take anymore. The need to take in big gulps of air and maybe pinch herself to make sure this was really happening was overwhelming. She said his name on a sigh and couldn't help but smile when he reared up and peeled off his suit jacket and tie. The only light in the room came from the fading sun coming through the blinds.

His eyes never left hers as both garments hit the floor. Then one hand rested on her knee and then began a slow journey upward, taking the hem of her dress with it. Tricia swallowed hard and licked her lips in anticipation. By the time his hand was on her hip, she let out a purr – desperate for more of his touch.

"Trish?" he whispered.

She couldn't speak. "Mmm…"

"Tell me this is what you want," he urged. "Or tell me to stop."

Was he kidding? Tell him to stop? Um, no. That wasn't going to happen. Not right now. Possibly not ever. "Don't stop," she said, forcing herself to speak. Her heart was racing as he sat perfectly still for what seemed like forever. She began to squirm under his intense gaze and just when she didn't think she could stand it another minute – the silence, the anticipation – he stood.

"Ryan?"

Leaning forward, he placed a finger over her lips and then straightened. Slowly, he unbuttoned his shirt and peeled it off. He toed off his shoes as he unbuckled his belt. As the minutes went by, the more overwhelmed Tricia became. It was a striptease in the most basic sense and yet, it was the sexiest thing she'd ever seen. Her fingers twitched with the need to touch him, to be skin to skin with him. When his trousers hit the floor and the only garment left on Ryan were dark boxer briefs, she nearly sent a prayer heavenward.

Ryan reached out a hand to her and pulled her to her feet. *Yeah!* She thought. *My turn!* Stepping in close to him she held her breath as he reached behind her and unzipped her dress. When his hands moved away, the dress slipped slightly, but caught on her breasts. His gaze strayed to where the fabric stopped and she heard the slight intake of breath.

This was it. It was all or nothing and right now, Tricia wanted it all.

With Ryan.

With a slight shimmy, the dress slid from her body and pooled at her feet. The strapless garment had allowed her to go braless and even as she stood before him in nothing more than panties and stilettos, she didn't feel embarrassed. It was the most natural thing in the world.

Slowly, Ryan's hand lifted and cupped one breast and she couldn't help but moan. "Don't stop."

Then, carefully, he maneuvered them until they were back down on the sofa – Tricia on her back, Ryan beside her. "Say it again," he said, placing tiny kisses along her arm, her shoulder, her collar bone.

She didn't need to ask for clarification. "Don't stop."

And he didn't.

Not for a very long time.

****

The room was dark now, only a sliver of moonlight shining through the blinds. Ryan's heart was racing. He felt like he'd run a marathon. And in a way, he had.

Good lord. Tricia had worn him out.

She was tucked in beside him on the massive couch, her head on his shoulder, her hand over his heart. And if he wasn't mistaken, she had dozed off. He envied that. His mind was racing right now and he'd give anything to be able to just turn it off and relax and regroup.

No such luck.

It was bound to happen, he supposed. But it certainly had the potential to complicate things, especially where Sean was concerned. As close as he and his brother were, Ryan was sure that Tricia was going to be an issue between them. He'd always known how protective Sean was of her and obviously still was, and Ryan had a feeling Sean wasn't going to take too kindly to this turn of events. In his mind, no one was going to be good enough for Tricia.

Not even Ryan.

Beside him, Tricia shifted and snuggled closer, her thigh wrapping around his. God, she felt good. In a perfect world he'd scoop her up in his arms and carry her upstairs to bed and spend the rest of the night making love to her. But he should have been on the road over a couple of hours ago. Hell, he should be home by now. As if sensing his thoughts, Tricia raised her head and looked at him. With her hair tousled and the sleepy expression on her face, it just made him ache for her more.

"Hey," she said softly.

"Hey, yourself." Unable to help himself, he skimmed a finger across her cheek before gently combing her hair away from her face. "Are you okay?" he asked softly.

Nodding, she gave him a weak smile. "Sorry I fell asleep."

Was she kidding? A few minutes ago he was envious of her ability to sleep and – the purely masculine side of him – actually felt proud of himself for exhausting her. "It's all right." They stayed like that – in the dark, neither of them speaking – for a few minutes. Finally, Ryan cleared his throat. "I'm going to get something to drink. Can I get you something?"

She smiled again. "That should be my line."

Kissing the top of her head, he moved to sit up. Before he stood, he reached along the back of the sofa and took the soft throw blanket she kept there and covered her. She was beyond temptation and if she stayed sprawled out and naked like that much longer, he definitely wasn't going to leave.

With her covered, he reached for his boxers and pulled them on before leaving the room. She technically hadn't answered him about wanting something to drink, but he'd bring her one anyway.

Once in the kitchen he paused and gave himself a moment to breathe and get his thoughts together. How was he supposed to get up and leave now? What did this mean for the two of them? While it may have seemed like he was just reacting to an emotionally-charged situation, the fact was he had wanted Tricia and didn't need any provocation. But what about her?

"Okay, don't overthink this," he murmured to himself as he pulled open the refrigerator door and grabbed a bottle of juice. He poured them each a glass and took a long drink of his and then poured himself a second glass.

Shit. He didn't want things to be awkward, not between him and Tricia and not between him and Sean. But he had no idea how to go about making sure that didn't happen. Placing the juice container back in the fridge, he sighed. Maybe it would be best if he got dressed and left. He was still coming back next weekend for the wedding and he'd certainly make the effort to talk to Trish during the week, but maybe a little distance was what he needed right now.

With that decided, he reached for the glasses, turned and froze. Tricia was standing in the doorway wrapped in the thin blanket he'd placed on her moments ago. Her shoulders were bare, her long, red hair doing little to cover any of her creamy skin. Ryan swallowed hard.

"You were gone a long time," she said softly. "I thought maybe you needed a hand."

A hand? Hell, he needed more than a hand; he needed all of her. And then the decision was made. He put the glasses back down on the counter and walked toward her and with very little effort, tugged the blanket from her grasp and watched it fall to the floor.

Tricia naked in the moonlight was quite possibly the most erotic sight he'd ever seen. He gently raked his hands through her hair and then let them skim down her arms until their fingers were twined. "Do you want some juice?"

She shook her head.

"Are you sure? I poured it, but…I got distracted."

She shook her head again. "It's not juice I want." And then she gave him a seductive grin and he said a quick prayer of thanks before scooping her up in his arms. He started toward the stairs when she stopped him. "I…I thought you needed to head home tonight." Her query was spoken softly, almost shyly.

"Sweetheart, I'm not going anywhere except up these stairs."

Her grin grew. "Thank God."

He took the stairs two at a time and didn't go back down until almost noon the next day.

****

When the phone rang early Wednesday morning, Tricia knew without even looking that it was Sean. And for the first time since they met, she was hesitant to answer.

It wasn't that she didn't want to talk to him – not really – but he just knew her so well she didn't think she'd be able to keep it from him that she'd slept with Ryan.

And just the thought of Ryan made her smile and blush and go hot all over.

Their night together had been amazing. Hot, steamy and wild one minute, sweet, slow and passionate the next. There had been very little sleeping and by the time Ryan had left, Tricia was lucky she could remember her own name. She'd worried about him driving all the way home on such little sleep, but he assured her he was fine.

He even called her when he'd gotten home to let her know he was all right. And they'd spoken every day – several times a day – since.

She sighed. It didn't seem possible. For all the years they'd known one another, she never imagined they would…fit quite like this. The upside was that because they'd known one another for so long, it did away with a lot of that new relationship awkwardness. They still didn't know each other very well – not like the way she knew Sean – so there was enough mystery about each other that they had so much to talk about and never seemed to run out of things to say.

She had fallen hard. Fast.

And it scared the hell out of her.

The phone was still ringing and she finally reached over and answered it. "Hey! How's my favorite patient doing today?"

"Grumpy."

"Oh, no," she cooed, knowing how much Sean loved sympathy. "What's going on? Who's not treating you right? Do I need to come and kick some nurse's ass?"

Sean chuckled. "As great as that would be – especially if you were both dressed in those short nurse's uniforms – no. I'm just antsy to get out of here and back home."

"I know, Sean. I wish they'd let you travel sooner. Your room is here waiting for you."

"Are you sure? I think Ryan's got it booked through the summer," he said with a laugh.

Tricia's heart began to race. Sean didn't know about her and Ryan, did he? Ryan hadn't mentioned telling him and Tricia knew she hadn't had the opportunity to bring it up. She cleared her throat. "What…what do you mean?" she asked nervously.

"The weddings," he said. "With him taking my place, I'm sure he's going to be there most weekends."

Oh, right. The weddings. She almost sagged to the floor with relief. "There aren't that many of them and he does have a place of his own so…"

"So you're saying my room is still available?"

She laughed. "You may have to share like the old days for a weekend of two, but otherwise you're fine."

"Can't you make him stay in the guest room?" he whined but Tricia knew he was just being cute.

"Actually, I think you should stay in the guest room so you don't have to maneuver the stairs. But we'll deal with that at a later date, like when we know you're coming home. Any word on that?"

"Nothing definitive." He paused. "So I haven't talked to you in a few days. How did the weekend go? Was it weird going with Ryan?"

"Not as weird as I thought it would be," she began evasively, then gave him almost all of the details of each wedding and got him caught up with all the people she saw and what was going on in their lives. "It was so good to see everyone again! Honestly, we laughed so much I almost hated to leave."

"That's great. And Ryan was okay? He didn't give you any grief about being there?"

"What do you mean?"

"You know how he is…he's not big on socializing. He's a workaholic. I'm thankful these things are on the weekend otherwise he probably would have turned me down flat when I asked him to go with you."

Here was her opening to address some things. "I appreciate you wanting to help me out, Sean, but…I kind of wish you would have talked to me first about this."

"Why? He was a jerk, wasn't he? What did he say – or do – to upset you? I'll call him and…"

"No!" she interrupted. "That's not it at all. It's just...dammit...I don't need a babysitter, Sean. And that's what I feel like you have him doing, watching over me and making sure I'm all right. Well, I am. I may not like it when people do the pity thing, but I get through it. And running into people I don't want to see? That's just a part of life."

He was silent for a moment. "So Steve was there."

Of course he would know what she was referring to. They'd known each other for so long that there wasn't anything they could get by one another. "Sunday. He was there and it was awkward and terrible at first, but then..."

"Please tell me you finally told him to get lost!"

"Actually, no."

"Tricia!" he snapped. "What is it going to take for you to realize what a jackass that guy is? How many more times..."

"I didn't get to tell him anything because Ryan took care of it," she said tartly.

"Oh," he said, sounding a bit sheepish. "Oh, okay. So...what did he say?" Tricia recounted the story to him and left it at their leaving the wedding – and not what happened once they got home. "Good. Maybe now Steve will finally get the hint and stop trying to get in touch with you."

"Well, if we're being honest, I probably should have been a little more firm with him from the beginning. If I had responded to his voicemails and texts telling him to back off, chances are we wouldn't have had any issues this weekend."

"Somehow I doubt that, but whatever."

"Anyway, the next wedding is this weekend and I told Ryan he didn't have to go with me." Actually, they had discussed it at great length but they both knew – especially after Sunday night – that he was coming back.

"I hope he told you it doesn't matter and he's going with you anyway."

She smiled. "Yeah. Something like that."

"Good." He sounded pleased. "I know it's not the same as us going together, but…I'm glad he's there with you."

"I told you. I don't need a babysitter," she said wearily.

"Yeah, yeah, yeah. Don't look at it like that. As much as it may seem like he's doing me a favor, the truth is, I'm kind of doing him one."

She frowned. "Meaning what, exactly?"

"Like I said, Ryan's a bit antisocial. The only time he really goes out and meets with people is when it's business related – dinners, drinks and whatnot. By going to the weddings with you, I feel good knowing he's out and about and mingling with people and he's not spending the night talking about architecture."

"Are you sure about that? For all you know that's all he talks about around the table. Maybe he's regaling everyone with talks about homes and buildings he's designed." She was teasing but did her best to keep her tone neutral.

"Please tell me you're kidding," Sean pleaded. "I will die of embarrassment if he's boring everyone to tears with talks of building materials and use of natural lighting."

Tricia burst out laughing. "Dammit! I wish I could have pulled that off a little bit longer!"

"You almost had me there for a minute," he said, laughing with her. "Not funny, Patterson!"

"You totally deserved that, Peterson," she replied. "Anyway, things are going fine. Ryan's going to be here this weekend."

"I have access to a computer," Sean said. "I'm going to try to Skype with you guys while he's there."

"That would be great! I can't wait to see your face!"

"Yeah, well, don't get too excited. It's still kind of bruised from the accident."

"Oh…Sean…"

"No worries. I'll be back to my adorable self by the time I come home."

She smiled and relaxed a bit. "I can't wait."

****

Late Friday afternoon, Ryan was pulling off the expressway and onto the exit that would lead him toward Tricia's house. He couldn't believe how anxious he was to get there. Not only had he essentially blown off work on Monday so he could stay in bed with her, but he'd left work early today in order to get back to her.

They'd talked on the phone every day and he found he simply enjoyed hearing her voice and learning more about her. The work she did as a speech pathologist was fascinating and the fact that she loved her job came through in everything she said. To think back and remember her as the shy girl Sean had brought home all those years ago was almost impossible. All he could see now was the beautiful and intelligent woman she'd become.

Technically, he didn't have to get to Tricia's until tomorrow since the wedding wasn't until Saturday night, but he didn't want to wait. He couldn't wait, actually. Even now, the drive itself was nearly killing him. As he drove through town, he thought about taking Tricia out to dinner and out on a proper date – just the two of them. Granted, they'd gone out to eat in the last couple of weeks, but that was more as friends or acquaintances. But now? Now it was different. He wanted to take her someplace romantic – maybe a little dancing afterwards.

Without a DJ and a hundred people dancing with them like at the weddings.

A smile crossed his face. Yes. That sounded like a great way to start the weekend. They'd go out and he'd show her a little romance – show her he was interested in her as more than something casual – and then they could go back to the house and have some ice cream out on the deck. He chuckled as he thought about how much she loved her favorite dessert. And then...then they could spend the night making love.

Maybe even start out on the deck.

The idea had merit.

He hit some traffic and couldn't help but curse. He was so close to Tricia's house that any delay was just flat-out annoying. The clock read four-thirty. She had mentioned she wouldn't be home until maybe a little after five and in his mind, Ryan had hoped to get to the house before her and surprise her, maybe have a couple of glasses of wine poured and waiting for her out on the deck. Looking over at the passenger seat, he looked at the bouquet of flowers he'd picked up for her and the bottle of his favorite wine he'd chosen, too.

His head shook. This was all new territory. He'd dated plenty of women in his life so that wasn't the new part. But he'd never had this kind of a history with one. They'd known each other for years and there was her relationship with not just Sean but his entire family. But even more than that, Ryan felt a deeper connection with Tricia than he ever had with a woman. It was hard to believe they hadn't gotten together sooner.

When?

Okay, yeah, there was that. Back when Sean first started bringing Tricia around, she was basically a child. She was in high school but compared to him, she was still a child. Plus, he went away for college and was only home occasionally and then moved to Jersey. So really, when had he actually had an opportunity to get to know her? The few times he'd seen her over the years was more in passing or in group settings. He had no idea that she was so…everything.

He cursed the slow-moving cars in front of him as he finally rolled through the intersection. Her neighborhood was only two blocks up and once he was off this main road, it would be smooth sailing.

His heart began to race as anticipation built. If it were possible for him to feel any more than what he was feeling at this moment, he couldn't comprehend it. Need. Want. It all warred within him. When her house was finally in sight, his foot pressed down harder on the gas pedal and he took the turn into the driveway almost on two wheels.

Tricia's car was nowhere in sight and he was thrilled that his plan was falling into place. Maybe once he got all his stuff inside, he'd put the car in the garage so she wouldn't have any idea he was inside waiting.

A slow smile crossed his face at the thought of the look on hers when she saw him.

With hands that were slightly trembling, he climbed out of the car and made quick work of collecting his things. He used his key to get in, felt only marginally guilty about doing so, and first went to the kitchen, dropping his suitcase next to the stairs. He found a vase for the flowers and got them set up with water. Then he searched her cabinets for wine glasses and put them on the counter next to the wine.

Striding back out to the foyer, he quickly scooped up his luggage and started up the stairs. In his mind he knew the right thing to do was to put his things in his old room, but part of him really just wanted to unpack in Tricia's and share the space with her for the weekend. Once he hit the landing, he paused.

"You're being stupid," he mumbled to himself. "Who cares where your luggage is?" Then he turned toward his room only to stop and look over his shoulder at the Tricia's closed door. Indecision warred within him for all of five seconds before he turned around and walked toward it. Maybe he was crossing a line, maybe he wasn't but there was only one way to find out.

Refusing to overanalyze it anymore, Ryan reached for the door handle and pushed the door open.

And found Tricia lying across the bed, draped only in a white sheet, waiting for him.

All thoughts of luggage were forgotten.

"What took you so long?" she asked, a sexy smile on her lips.

And in that moment, he had to wonder the exact same thing.

Seven

They lay facing one another a bit later on, Ryan's fingers trailing up and down Tricia's arm. "I was hoping to surprise you," she said.

"That had been my plan too," he said with a low chuckle and then looked up into her eyes. "One mind."

"Mm-hmm," she purred and sighed. Closing her eyes, Tricia could easily picture the look on Ryan's face when he'd come through her bedroom door earlier. Shock and then heat. She loved that look. Reaching up, she traced a finger along his stubbled jaw and was content for them to just stay like this. She was just about to say that when he moved and pushed the sheet off of them. "What are you doing?"

Ryan stood and then took one of her hands in his and pulled her to her feet. With a wicked look in his eyes, he gently tugged her along – out of the bedroom, down the hall and into the bathroom. He turned the water on in the shower and then turned to face her. "I want to take you to dinner tonight and right now, neither of us is fit to go anywhere."

With a tilt of her head she gave him a wry look. "And you think having us shower together will help that?"

"It certainly can't hurt, sweetheart."

Who was she to argue?

They stepped under the steamy spray and it wasn't long before Tricia found out she had seriously underestimated the appeal of a shared shower.

Ryan's hands were felt like they were everywhere at once and she found he was extremely creative in how he used them. It didn't matter how much soap they used, she felt a little dirtier – and naughtier – than she had after their romp in her bed!

The water was turning cool when he turned it off and reached for a towel for her, wrapping her in it. He placed a kiss on her forehead and wrapped his arms around her. "Where should we go for dinner?"

Dinner? He could think about food right now? Her knees were weak and her heart was still racing. "I'd be happy with a pizza out on the deck."

He chuckled. "I'll admit right now that does sound good, but I really wanted to take you out someplace."

Tricia pulled back and looked up at him. "You don't have to do that. We went out the last two times you were here. I really don't mind staying in."

Leaning down, he kissed her thoroughly. "I don't either," he murmured against her lips, "but if we stay in, I don't think we'll ever get to dinner."

"And that's a bad thing?" Tricia took a step back and grabbed a towel and handed it to him.

"Woman, I'm starving already. We'll at least need a snack," he teased, wrapping the towel around his waist as he followed her out of the bathroom and back to her room.

Tricia noticed a blinking light on her phone. "I must have missed a call while we were in there," she murmured, picking it up and connecting to her voicemail. After a minute, she went, "Uh-oh..."

"What? What's the matter?"

She held up a finger to stop him and finished listening. When she hung up, she looked at him, slightly dismayed.

"Who was on the phone? Is everything all right?" he asked.

"That was your mom," she began. "She's on her way here." Tricia looked over at her clock. "Actually, she should be here in about twenty minutes."

And there went their romantic dinner plans.

****

Ryan put the wine glasses away and put the vase of flowers on the dining room table and sighed, best laid plans and all.

He couldn't believe his mother was on her way here, but that was the kind of woman she was. She pretty much did what she wanted, when she wanted and didn't bother to check and see if it was convenient for anyone else.

Disappointment swamped him. Not that he didn't want to see his mother – it had been months since he had – it's just he would have preferred to see her at another time.

Like any time other than tonight.

As soon as Tricia had told him the news, they sprang into action. He had quickly gotten dressed and come downstairs while Tricia dried her hair and got herself dressed. It wasn't the way he envisioned them getting ready but it couldn't be helped.

He heard the slam of a car door and knew his mother had arrived. The smile came easily as he walked to the door, pulled it open and waited for her.

"Ryan!" she said with delight. "I had no idea you'd be here this weekend! What a wonderful surprise!"

"Hey, Mom," he said, kissing her on the cheek. He held the door open for her and then followed her into the house and into the living room.

"Where's Tricia?" she asked, looking around the room and smiling.

"She's getting changed. Your call took her by surprise and she just wanted to freshen up."

"Oh, she didn't have to go through any trouble for me," Steph said. "Look at how wonderful the house looks. I can't believe how she's kept so much of it the same. I would have thought she would want to get rid of some of this old stuff. I know I did!"

Ryan laughed. "She claims she loves it all."

"She's just being sweet."

Ryan couldn't help but agree, but he had to be careful about how he acted right now. He and Tricia hadn't really talked about where they saw their relationship going, and Ryan had a feeling if his mother caught wind of what was going on, she'd butt in and start pushing them toward things they might not be ready for.

"Tricia!" Steph cried boisterously as Tricia entered the living room. The two women embraced as Ryan stood back and observed. "Look at you! You get prettier and prettier every time I see you!" She gave Tricia another hug and then looked over her shoulder. "Don't you agree, Ryan?"

Rather than answer, Ryan walked toward the kitchen. "Would you like something to drink, Mom?"

"That would be lovely," she said, taking Tricia by the hand and following him. "Everything looks wonderful, Tricia. It's always such a good feeling when I walk through that door. I know I didn't want to live here anymore but there is something very comforting in being able to come back every once in a while. So thank you."

Tricia blushed. "You don't need to thank me. I've told you about a hundred times how much I love this house. It's comforting to me too." She reached out and took the glass of wine from Ryan's hand, giving him a curious look.

"Oh that's good," Steph said after taking a sip. "You have excellent taste in wine." It was directed toward Tricia and neither she nor Ryan corrected her. Looking at her son, she relaxed against the kitchen counter. "So what brings you here, Ryan? Working in the area?"

Ryan looked at Tricia and she shrugged and gave him the go-ahead. "Actually, I'm subbing for Sean."

Steph looked at him and then Tricia and then back again. "Excuse me?"

"Why don't we go sit down and explain it to you?" Tricia suggested and led Steph back to the living room where they sat down on the sofa. For the next few minutes, she described to Steph the wedding season plan.

"So…you and Sean were supposed to go together as a fake couple?" she asked and Tricia nodded. "But because of the accident, Ryan's going with you?"

Tricia nodded again.

"Interesting," Steph said and took a sip of her wine. "So how believable are you?"

"We seem to be doing okay," Tricia answered. "No one has doubted us for a moment. It was kind of funny watching their expressions at that first wedding when we made our announcement, but for the most part, no one's the wiser." Tricia paused, waiting for Ryan to add something to the conversation. When he didn't, she continued. "Anyway, we have another wedding tomorrow and then one early in July, one at the end, and one in August. For all I know, more invitations can be on the way."

"Wow, that's a lot of weddings," Steph said, smiling at her son. "Good for you for stepping in and helping out. I know how much you hate these kinds of social events."

Ryan rolled his eyes. "I don't hate them, Mom. I just choose not to go to them."

"And why is that?" she prompted.

He frowned at her. "Because I don't overly enjoy them."

"That's just a nicer way of saying you hate them," she said with a knowing grin. She patted him on the knee. "Like I said, it was nice of you to step in and help out. Not that I think our girl here couldn't handle herself on her own, but my goodness…all those weddings in one summer. You could have said no to some of them," she said to Tricia.

"I had thought the same thing at first, but the more Sean and I talked about it, we couldn't figure out whose we would skip."

"I would imagine it would have been tough," Steph said, taking another sip of her wine. "And if I know Sean, he waxed poetic about who he was friends with in high school and for how long and how it wouldn't be right for him not to be there."

"Exactly!" Tricia laughed. "And so far, I've had a great time with everyone we've seen and I hate that Sean's missing it."

"I know he is too, sweetie," Steph sighed. "I hate not being with him and it's even worse not knowing exactly when he's going to come home." She paused.

112

"Which reminds me, has anyone talked to him about where he's going to stay when that happens?"

Tricia ducked her head shyly and then raised her hand. "I did," she said. "I told him he could stay here if he needed to." She looked at Steph apologetically. "I know I probably should have talked to you first but...I don't know. I know you travel a lot and I have all this space here so..."

Steph took one of Tricia's hands in hers and squeezed. "Don't be silly. It does make the most sense. I could easily rearrange my schedule so he could stay with me but my place is really just a studio. He'd have no privacy. This makes the most sense." She looked over at Ryan. "Unless you'd like him to stay with you?"

Ryan shook his head. "I travel too much. Tricia's right. Here he can use the guest room and with her work schedule, she could be here to help him if he needs it."

Steph nodded and leaned over to kiss her son on the cheek. "Plus, if she really needed your help, I know you'd be here."

He nodded.

"So what did the two of you have planned for tonight? Anything? Because I'd love to take you both out to dinner!" Steph smiled at them both. "I had planned on having some girl time with Tricia but finding Ryan here was such a wonderful surprise! I feel like we need to go out and celebrate a bit."

"Celebrate? Celebrate what?" Ryan asked.

"Whatever we feel like!" Steph answered. "Come on. Give me five minutes to freshen up and we can go into town for something to eat."

"You're going to stay the night aren't you, Steph?" Tricia asked.

"Oh, heavens no. You were actually just a bit of a pit stop for me. Sorry," she said with a sincere smile. "I'm actually driving out to the Hamptons tonight and meeting up with some friends."

"Tonight?" Ryan asked. "You'll be getting there kind of late. Why don't you just stay here and drive out in the morning?"

"Because traffic will be a beast then. Trust me. I've done this dozens of times before. We'll grab some dinner, visit and catch up with one another and then I'll be on my way."

"I wish you'd reconsider," Tricia added.

"That's sweet of the both of you but I'll be fine. Give me five minutes. In the meantime, think of where you'd like to go to eat."

When she was out of the room, Ryan stood and looked at Tricia. "Not the evening I had planned for us."

She stood as well. "It's okay, we have all weekend. It will be nice to visit with her for a little while."

He leaned in and kissed her – although kiss was too mild a word. Devoured was more like it. It left her weak and achy and needy. When he released her, she almost lost her balance. "No fair."

He smirked. "What? What's no fair?"

"How am I supposed to focus on dinner after that?"

"You're not. You're supposed to focus on what comes later on."

As if she'd be able to think of anything else.

****

Once at the restaurant – a local Irish pub – they ordered food, ate and talked almost non-stop. There never seemed to be a lull in the conversation and the only thing missing was Sean. Tricia had always enjoyed spending time with the Petersons. They offered her the kind of relaxed family atmosphere that had been missing in her own life.

Meeting Sean on her first day of school here had been the burst of fresh air she had needed. And now, sitting here with Ryan and Steph – and Sean in spirit – filled her heart with love.

Her gaze lingered on Ryan. He looked so relaxed as he talked about the new office complex he was designing. He was very expressive when he spoke of his work and she knew how much he loved his work. She'd always known what he did, but it wasn't until recently she realized just how much he did and how talented he was. Out of the corner of her eye, she caught Steph watching her and quickly turned her focus to her food.

When their dinner plates were cleared, Steph ordered dessert for them to share. "I know we all say we're full, but there's always room for dessert," she said.

Tricia leaned back in her seat, her hand over her belly. "I don't know about that. It's like that at the weddings, too. Between the cocktail hour and all the food at the reception, by the time the cake comes out and all the assorted desserts, it's almost painful."

"Nonsense," Steph said. "There's nothing wrong with indulging once in a while." She clapped her hands with glee when the plates came out – cheesecake, pecan pie and death-by-chocolate.

Any time she had ever gone out to eat with Steph, it had been with Sean. They all shared their desserts and it was all done in good fun – feeding one another and critiquing their choices. But when Steph suggested Tricia feed Ryan a piece of her chocolate cake, Tricia wasn't so sure she'd be able to do it and have it look all that platonic.

"She doesn't have to feed me, Mom," Ryan said, clearly thinking the same thing. He reached across the table with his fork to get a piece but Steph smacked his hand away.

"That's not how we do it. We have a thing we do – of course, it's when Sean is with us – but you'll just have to go with the flow."

Tricia looked at him apologetically as she lifted a forkful of the decadent dessert and held it to his lips. He slowly took it into his mouth and she almost groaned, unable to look away. Ryan's eyes held hers and she could feel the flush creeping up her body and every inch of her body tingled in anticipation – as if he was actually touching her.

Suddenly remembering Steph was sitting there watching them, she quickly pulled the fork away and cleared her throat.

"I know you're not a huge fan of cheesecake, Trish," Steph said, "but you really need to try Ryan's. The pub is famous for it."

"No, that's okay…"

"Oh, come on!" Steph said with a grin, "You know the rules. Everyone has to taste."

It was normally a fun tradition but right now it was beginning to feel like torture. As much as Tricia loved spending time with Stephanie Peterson, right now she wouldn't mind if she wanted to get on the road to the Hamptons.

With another apologetic look, Tricia waited for Ryan to feed her a piece of his dessert. As much as she told herself to act natural and not focus on his face, she couldn't. It was as if she was completely incapable of looking anyplace else. She took the forkful of the creamy dessert and when Ryan slowly pulled the fork away, she caught his heated grin.

"Both of those must be spectacular, judging by your faces!" Steph said with a chuckle and then reached over and took a taste of each on her own.

"Hey!" both Tricia and Ryan said in unison.

"What?"

"You broke the rules!" Tricia laughed. "Why did we have to feed each other and you got to just swoop in and taste on your own?"

"Because I'm the mom and therefore I get to do what I want!" They all laughed and finished their desserts. Once the check was paid, Steph stood and stretched. "I really hate to eat and run, but it is getting late. I hope you don't mind me cutting the night short."

Tricia had never been more thankful for anything in her life and by the look on Ryan's face, it was mutual.

"Not a problem," Ryan said as they made their way back out to the car.

Back at the house, they said their goodbyes out in the driveway with Steph promising to text them when she arrived at her friend's house. Tricia stood next to Ryan as they watched his mother drive away, keenly aware of his hand resting on the small of her back.

"Well that was a nice surprise," she said as Steph's car disappeared down the road.

"Absolutely. But in typical mom-fashion, she's here and gone in a flash and somehow never really manages to tell you what's going on in her life or what she's up to."

"No, that's not true," Trish began to argue and then stopped and thought about it. "Actually…"

Ryan nodded. "You know I'm right. She had both of us talking about work and the weddings and then we talked about Sean but through it all, she said very little about her own life. She makes me crazy."

"Maybe she doesn't have a whole lot going on and thinks we don't want to hear about it?"

Now he shook his head. "No, I just think she enjoys her independence and doesn't want any of us to know what she's up to for fear we'll disagree with it or tell her to stop doing what she's doing."

"Oh, come on, Ry. What could she possibly be doing that you or Sean would tell her to stop?"

"With her? You never know. She's getting more and more adventurous in her old age and I don't think she realizes she's not as young as she used to be."

"There's nothing wrong with that," Tricia countered. "I say good for her. I hope she's having fun with it."

"And if she gets hurt?" he said a little defensively.

Looking at him, Tricia rolled her eyes playfully. "Ryan, she's a grown woman and really, we all have the ability of getting hurt. Are you suggesting she should just stay home and be bored for the rest of her life?"

He looked like he was going to argue and then thought better of it. He maneuvered himself so they were facing one another and then wrapped his arms around her waist. "As much as I enjoy bantering with you – even if it's in the middle of your driveway – I would much rather take this inside."

She smiled knowingly and nodded, taking him by the hand and leading him to the door. Once inside, she only flipped on the foyer light before walking toward the kitchen. "I forgot to thank you for the wine earlier. It really was great."

"Thanks. I had bought it for us to share before dinner – out on the deck. But then mom called and…"

"It's quite all right," she said, suddenly noticing the vase on the table. "Flowers? You bought flowers too? Why didn't you say anything?"

"In front of my mother? Could you imagine how much different the night would have gone if she had any idea I'd bought you wine and flowers? We would have gotten the third-degree all night long!" He laughed at the image. "You know how she gets, Trish. As it is I think she was kind of on to us with that whole dessert thing. Do you guys really feed each other dessert when you go out?"

She nodded. "It started out innocently enough years ago and then she made it a thing. But tonight? I think you're right. She was looking a bit pleased with herself during it all."

"And that's without her really knowing anything. If we had told her we are…involved, she would have certainly started pressing to see how serious we are and what our plans are for the future and whatever else goes with that."

Tricia wouldn't mind finding some of that out for herself.

Unsure of what to do with herself, she leaned against the counter and looked at him. "I was about to ask if you wanted anything to eat or drink but the thought of either of those things is making me a little green."

He chuckled. "I know what you mean." Then he approached – slowly – and caged her in, bracketing his arms on either side of her. "This was a little more of what I had in mind for when we came back from dinner."

"Really?" she asked softly, looking up at him.

"Mmm-hmm," he said, leaning down and nuzzling her neck. "My plan had been for us to have a drink out on the deck before dinner, and then I was going to take you out someplace romantic. Then we'd come back here – just like this – and go and sit out on the deck for a little while."

"I like the sound of that."

Stepping back, Ryan smiled at her and walked over to the French doors and opened them. He stood and waited for her to join him.

It was the perfect evening, plenty of stars in the sky and a gentle breeze blowing. Ryan led her to one of the chaise lounges before going back inside. Tricia thought of questioning him but decided to wait and see what he was doing. Two minutes later he was back with a glass of wine for each of them, but he never turned on any of the outside lights.

"I managed to make sure there was enough for us to have a little when we got home," he said, handing her the glass.

When she sat up, Ryan swung a leg around and lowered himself behind her. She leaned back against him and sighed. "Now this is a good plan."

His lips instantly went to her throat and she merely tilted her head to give him better access. "It's about to get a whole lot better."

"Oh, really?" she purred.

He nodded against her. "How private is this yard?"

"Extremely," she said on a sigh. "I think."

"Are you willing to find out?"

And as his hand began to roam all over her body, she would have willingly agreed to just about anything. "Out here? Really?"

"Do you trust me?"

Him? Absolutely. Herself? Not so much.

Slowly he began to unbutton the sleeveless blouse she wore and gently opened it. His hands cupped her lace-covered breasts and he let out a low growl of appreciation. She sighed his name.

"You'll have to be very quiet," he murmured, his hands teasing her into a frenzy.

Rather than argue, Tricia managed to turn in his arms so his lips could replace his hands. This time his growl was a little less than quiet. She chuckled. "Same rules apply," she whispered huskily.

And it was the last words either uttered for a long time.

Eight

After the wedding Saturday, there wasn't another one for almost a month. It was sort of the elephant in the room when Ryan was getting ready to leave the next day.

"So…the eleventh, right?" he asked, looking at his calendar.

Tricia nodded.

That was a lot longer than he wanted and his schedule was pretty packed in between, which is what he told her.

"Ryan," she began, "it's okay. We both have lives and you live three hours away. It wasn't like our sleeping together was going to change that."

He knew she was going for casual but for some reason, hearing her describing what they were doing as merely sleeping together made him uncomfortable. They were sharing breakfast out on the deck and the thought of leaving was unappealing, but what else was new?

"Why don't you come by me next weekend? I can show you my neck of the woods," he suggested and was relieved when she smiled at him.

"Are you sure? I know you have a very busy schedule and I don't want to interfere. I've already disrupted your time enough with these silly weddings."

Taking one of her hands in his, he squeezed. "Well, these silly weddings were the best thing that could have happened." He waited until her eyes met his. "I mean it, Tricia. I know I wasn't on board with all of it in the beginning but now? Now that we've had the time to get to know each other, I'm really glad things worked out like this." Then he stopped and chuckled. "Not that I'm happy about Sean getting hurt, but…you know."

She nodded. "I know exactly what you mean. It's just…well…we live so far apart. I'm sure it's going to be difficult and then it will just get old – commuting back and forth. And…"

He placed a finger over her lips to stop her. "Let's not think about that right now, okay? For now, let's just enjoy what we have and take it one day at a time, okay?"

Ryan noticed a hint of sadness in her eyes but refused to comment on it. Instead he kissed the back of her hand and turned the conversation toward more neutral topics. "It was good to see Sean this morning."

Earlier, as promised, Sean had used a computer to Skype with them. She nodded. "He looks way too thin. I can't wait for him to get home so he can heal properly and get back to his old self."

Honestly, Ryan had been more than a little dismayed by his brother's appearance but it still had been good to actually see his face while they talked. "Be careful what you wish for," he said with a smile. "He'll have you running all over town for his favorite foods or have you cooking at all hours of the day and night if he knows you're worried about him like that."

"Oh, please. Sean would never…" Then she stopped and thought about it. "Never mind. You're right. I'll just have to make sure the pantry is well stocked."

"Good girl."

"Hopefully we'll be able to get an actual return date out of him soon. I hate all this waiting around for answers."

He couldn't help but laugh a little. "You're not big on patience though either."

She gave him a wry look. "Seriously? You're going to talk to me about patience?"

He knew exactly what she was referring to, what they both were referring to. "Sweetheart, where you're concerned, I definitely don't have patience. When I think about you and how much I want you, I almost can't wait to have you." His voice was low and possessive and he loved the way his words made her blush.

Standing, Tricia gave a long, sensual stretch before looking at him. She was wearing a snug tank top and a tiny pair of shorts. "How's your patience level right now?"

Ryan kicked the chair out from under him in his haste to get to her. Without a word he lunged and swung her over his shoulder.

"Ryan!" she cried, laughing the entire time. "What in the world are you doing?"

He walked them into the house and was halfway up the stairs before he spoke. "I'm more demonstrative," he finally said. "I mean, I could tell you where my patience level was at, but I think it would be a whole heck of a lot more fun to just show you."

In her room, he playfully tossed her down onto the bed. He was peeling off his shirt before she even finished bouncing on the mattress.

"I do like a man of action," she cooed, her eyes watching as each piece of clothing was tossed aside.

"And that's why we're perfect together," he said before covering her body with his and kissing her senseless.

****

For the next month, they alternated weekends – one weekend in Jersey, the next back on the island. When it was time for wedding number four, they had pretty much established a bit of a routine.

Ryan would arrive on Friday afternoon, they'd go out to dinner, and then spend some time Skyping with Sean before they went to bed. Tricia was growing increasingly frustrated with her friend. She couldn't understand why he wasn't fighting harder for a release date from the hospital and coming home. Both Ryan and Steph seemed to agree with her, but

Sean would only say that whenever he found out, he'd let them know.

Saturday morning, Tricia reluctantly got out of bed, kissing Ryan on the cheek.

"Where are you going?"

"My usual spa appointment. I had hoped to do it yesterday but my afternoon appointment ran over. So I'm going to get all pampered and pretty for tonight."

He grinned at her. "You don't need all that stuff, you know. You're beautiful."

She blushed. "And you're very sweet for saying so but I'm never going to say no to a good mani/pedi."

Shaking his head, he rolled over in the bed. "I don't even want to know what that is."

"Go back to sleep and I'll be back in time for lunch."

Once she was out in the car, Tricia let out a little happy sigh. She was excited about tonight's wedding. Not that it was anything different from the previous ones, but it was the time she got to spend with Ryan that she was most looking forward to.

With their weekends together, they spent their time relaxing and just enjoying being with one another, but tonight? Tonight she'd get to dress up, dance with him and step out of their normal routine.

The dress she had purchased for the wedding was a little daring for her – strapless and cut above the knee in sapphire blue. There was a slit in the side that showed even more leg. The dress was so snug that only the tiniest of thongs would work with it. She thought of how Ryan would look at her and shivered.

They were more than halfway through this silly plan for the wedding season and once it was over, she couldn't help but wonder where they'd stand. While Ryan had encouraged her to let things go one day at a time, it just wasn't in her nature. She was a planner, a list maker. Making plans for her future was something she worked on daily. Once they didn't have the weddings hanging over them, where would they be?

For the last month they'd made it work, but it was a bit exhausting to keep it up, probably more so for Ryan. Although the nature of Tricia's job had her driving to her clients, Ryan's job and clients had him traveling farther distances. It certainly wasn't ideal for either of them to spend a large portion of their weekends driving to one another.

Don't go there.

Pushing the thought aside, she focused on getting to Starbucks and grabbing herself something yummy and then the glorious hours of pampering she had ahead.

****

They were dancing to a slow song at the reception later that evening. Ryan pulled her closed and whispered in her ear, "You look incredible. Have I mentioned that?"

Actually, he had.

Multiple times.

But this was the first time he'd said it so intimately, his hot breath and the tone of his voice giving her the shivers she'd imagined earlier. One large hand was placed possessively at the base of her spine and made her feel very warm. As usual, she couldn't wait for the end of the party when they could leave. As much as she loved celebrating with her friends, she loved being alone with Ryan even more.

When the music ended, they walked back to their table and chatted with friends. Everyone asked about Sean and when Tricia mentioned how they were currently Skyping with him, they talked about trying to use the app to get him on the phone so they could all see him.

"I…I'm honestly not sure if I know how to do that," Tricia said. And before she knew it, someone had her phone and was installing the app and then everyone was encouraging her to make the call. Looking over at Ryan, he simply smiled and shrugged so she figured why not?

It took a little while for the call to go through but then there he was – a big smile on his face and a warm greeting and once he realized where she was, he seemed to brighten up even more. "This is freaking awesome!" he said. "Come on, pass the phone around! Let me talk to everyone!"

So Tricia handed the phone off and rested her head on Ryan's shoulder.

"Hey," he said softly. "You okay?"

She nodded. "I wish I had thought of this sooner. Maybe if I had done this from the beginning, he'd be more anxious to come home."

He kissed the top of her head. "He is anxious to come home. It's just that he's in another country and he's seriously hurt. The doctors want to make sure he's okay to travel and his injuries are healed enough for it. You can't take it personally."

"I don't, I just...I don't know. Maybe I am. I just wish he were here and everything was back to normal."

Ryan stiffened beside her.

"What?" she asked softly. "What's the matter?"

He shook his head. "Nothing." His tone was light and his smile didn't quite reach his eyes.

Someone called their names and when they turned, her phone was being held up and Sean was looking at them. "You two are adorable!" Sean said with a grin. "It's nice to see you out and about together. Don't you guys all think they're adorable together?" He asked the group at the table. After a collective "yes," he put his attention back on Tricia and Ryan. "I'm seriously happy for the two of you."

Tricia knew Sean well enough to know he was up to something. She saw it in his eyes as a trickle of unease made its way down her spine. What in the world was he going to do?

"Which makes me wonder," he said, his grin growing. "When will we all be sitting around a table celebrating your wedding?"

She didn't have to look at Ryan to know he was shocked by Sean's question and Tricia was certain she'd lost every ounce of color in her face. Soon, everyone at the table was inquiring about their future and all Tricia could do was stare mutely at the telephone screen. This was exactly the sort of thing she was hoping to avoid by having a date and Sean knew it! She couldn't believe he'd say something so stupid!

Sean started to laugh. "Aww...don't be shy. I didn't mean to put you on the spot like that. Tell you what, since I haven't had the chance to hang out with you two since you started dating, let me just see you kiss and I'll drop all talk about any future wedding. What do you say?"

Tricia wanted to strangle him! What was wrong with him? She was just about to stand up and reach for the phone when Ryan spun her around and hauled her into his lap. "Ryan...what the...?"

She never got to finish. His lips claimed hers in a kiss so hot, so sensual that she almost melted to the floor from the pure heat of it. His tongue plundered, his hand anchored into her hair as the other held her securely against him. Everything in her clamored to wrap around him – even with the audience – but she managed to hold on to an ounce of dignity and just kiss him back as if her life depended on it.

When the wolf whistles and howls began to die down, Ryan lifted his head. His eyes were glazed and he gave her a look that promised pure sin when he had her alone. Carefully, he helped Tricia back into her chair and then he stood and reached for the phone. "Tell everyone goodnight, little brother." His voice was calm – almost too calm – and Tricia knew he was angry.

"It was great to see everyone! I promise to get in touch when I'm back in the States!" Sean said and then grinned when it was just Tricia and Ryan looking at him. "So...having fun?"

Tricia was aware there were still a lot of people looking at them and gently nudged Ryan. "If you don't mind, Sean," she said sweetly, "I think they're getting ready to cut the cake. We'll talk to you soon, okay?" And before he could answer, Ryan had hung up.

He handed her the phone and joined the conversation around the table, which had turned to sports. For a few minutes, she was happy to simply sit back and listen but her mind kept going back to Sean. Why would he embarrass them like that?

Her thoughts were interrupted by the DJ announcing the bride and groom were indeed ready to cut the cake. This filled her with relief because she was definitely ready for this night to end. She had a feeling Ryan was merely holding his tongue where his brother was concerned until after they left the wedding and were alone. It really wasn't a conversation she was looking forward to. She had primed and planned so much for this night and she wanted to strangle Sean for ruining it.

Once dessert was done, Ryan looked at her. "You ready?"

She nodded and put her hand in his when he stood. They made their rounds through the room and said their goodbyes, explaining how Ryan was leaving in the morning to head back to New Jersey and they wanted to get home early. No one held them up because they clearly thought they wanted to be alone.

The whole time they walked around, Ryan's hand was always possessively on either her back or hip and when they were finally outside and walking toward his car, it seemed to be urging her forward. They didn't speak the entire way home and the air around them seemed to crackle with tension. When they pulled into the driveway and parked the car, Ryan suddenly seemed incredibly calm.

Casually, he walked around to Tricia's door and helped her out and they walked quietly to the door. She felt extremely anxious and seemed unable to draw a complete breath. When she preceded him into the house, she was unsure of where she should go or what she should do. In her mind, she had everything planned for how she wanted the night to go, but after the whole Skyping thing with Sean, she sort of felt like they should at least talk about it.

Turning, she watched as Ryan closed and locked the door and shut off the outside light. Bathed in nothing but the moonlight, Tricia took a steadying breath. "I wish I knew why Sean…"

Ryan's mouth on hers stopped her from saying anything else. Clearly he didn't want to talk about it and for right now, Tricia was more than okay with that. For now she'd let herself forget about the awkward conversation and go back to her original plan for the night. Although with the way things were moving along right now, she wasn't going to get to seduce Ryan at all; he was the one intent on seducing her.

Lifting his head from hers, she felt his hand skim along her jaw right before he scooped her up in his arms and began climbing the stairs. Tricia rested her head on his shoulder and smiled. This was so much better than having a conversation about…well…anything.

For tonight, she'd be happy to converse with Ryan through nothing more than the touch of her hand and the sound of her sighs.

****

"I'm not going home today," Ryan said the next morning while Tricia was sprawled across his chest.

She lifted her head and looked at him. "How come?"

He sighed. Long after Tricia had fallen asleep, he'd stared at the ceiling thinking about Sean's behavior on the phone. Something wasn't right. The entire situation wasn't right and Ryan was determined to get to the bottom of it.

"I think I want to go and visit my mom."

Tricia looked at him in confusion. "Really? Where is she at these days? I haven't talked to her since we went to dinner with her last month."

"Yeah, she's been a little hard to pin down but she mentioned during one of our very brief phone conversations she was going to her place on Fire Island."

"What? But…that's so close by. Why would she go there and not call? We always get together when she's over there." She sat up. "I mean…I know she doesn't *have* to invite me, but ever since I started renting the house, that was something we always did."

Ryan nodded. "Exactly. And she knew I was going to be here too for some of the time and she's always pestering me about not visiting enough. So why is she being so secretive? Why all the radio silence all of a sudden?"

"Do you really think she's still over there? Maybe she only went for a day?"

"Between her weird behavior and Sean's, I don't know what's going on. But I can at least go and talk to her in person and get a little insight into all of it. I have no choice but to wait until Sean's back here in the States."

"I don't know what got into him last night. It could have just been him having a little fun at our expense, but…"

This time he shook his head. "No. Something's off. He's another one who's being secretive. If he's seriously stuck over there for all this time, there's no reason why no one should have gone to see him. If Mom and I were willing to take the time, she should have been happy to have us there. I think something's wrong." He stopped for a minute. "I mean, more serious than he's letting on."

Tricia gasped. "Do you really think so?"

"Why else isn't he home yet or letting us come to him? You know how he is, Trish. He loves the attention and to be a little pampered. It goes with him being the baby of the family. If we were willing to go over there and make a fuss over him, why didn't he let us?"

"Hmm…I never thought of it like that."

"And I think Mom knows more than she's letting on."

She looked at him sympathetically. "I think you're making more of this than you need to. Maybe Sean just thought he was being funny? Maybe Steph is dating or something and doesn't want us hanging around? This could all be a bunch of nothing."

"If it is, then all we have to lose is a ferry ride back and forth to Fire Island. Come on. What do you say? We'll make a day of it."

He saw the indecision on her face, the way she was gently biting her bottom lip. Sitting up, he kissed her and kept on kissing her until she melted against him and agreed to go with him.

It was almost lunchtime when they finally boarded the ferry. Now, as they sat up on the top deck, they silently stared out at the water.

Ryan was lost in his own thoughts, and they were going in a dozen different directions. For a while now, his weekends were all about his time with Tricia. Sure there were the weddings, but for the most part he saw the weekends as their time. Right now, he almost resented the fact that reality had interrupted. Even though this was about his mother – and his brother – it didn't make it any easier.

Then it was back to Tricia. When Sean had made that stupid comment last night about when it was going to be their wedding, at first Ryan was shocked, then a little bit angry that his brother was clearly being a troublemaker, and then…nothing. The thought of a future with Tricia – marrying Tricia – didn't make him freak out. At thirty-two, he was fine with the idea of settling down; it was just that up until now, he hadn't met anyone he wanted to settle down with.

Until Tricia.

He knew Sean's comments bothered her. He wasn't exactly sure why, and maybe he should have spent a little more time this morning talking to her about it. Unfortunately, he was a man of action and with so many things bothering him, he felt like his mother would be the easiest of them all. She was accessible and in all his life they'd never had a disagreement that ended badly.

Sean was too far away to deal with.

And Tricia may very well tell him she didn't feel the same way he did.

So, going to his mother's place was also the safest place to start.

They docked and made the twenty-minute walk to the small house Steph had on the island. She rented it out for most of the summer but Ryan was hoping he hadn't misunderstood her during their last conversation.

Beside him, Tricia walked along silently. He held her hand but she seemed perfectly content to keep things quiet. It was one of the things he really was becoming to love about her – she understood him. He could have easily carried on a conversation but right now it just seemed better for him to keep his thoughts straight so he'd know what to say when they got to the house.

Sure enough, when the house came into view, Steph was out in the yard talking to someone. For a minute, Ryan hesitated. Then he realized it was one of her neighbors and put a smile on his face.

"You ready for this?" Tricia asked quietly.

"I hope so," he replied honestly. "Believe me, I hope you're right and I'm just making more out of all of this than there actually is. Unfortunately, I don't think I am."

As they approached the small white picket fence, Steph turned. Her first reaction was a bit of wide-eyed shock, then her face eased into a smile. "Ryan! Tricia! What are you two doing here? Is there a wedding on the island today?"

They both walked over and kissed her. "Nope, the wedding was last night," Ryan said. "But I thought I remembered you saying something about being here and we decided to take a chance and surprise you so…surprise!"

"How sweet of you! How about some lunch?" Steph asked and then started toward the house. "Just give me two minutes to grab my purse and we'll go and grab something."

"We just had breakfast a little while ago," Ryan said. "We really just came by to visit. Let's go inside and get out of the sun."

"What?" Steph cried. "Um…no. I mean, why don't we go down by the beach?"

Ryan wasn't going to be swayed. He hooked his arm smoothly through his mother's and turned her back toward the house. "You know Tricia is fair-skinned. She burns easily. I'm sure she would love to be out of the sun for a little while."

Steph looked a bit uncomfortable but finally caved. She opened the front door and ushered them in. "Have a seat. I'll just go and grab us some drinks."

When she was out of sight, Ryan sat down and motioned for Tricia to do the same. "I think that was all a little suspicious."

"I have to agree," Tricia whispered. "You mother is one of the most hospitable people I know." She looked around the room and then back at Ryan. "Why wouldn't she want us here?"

Nothing was obvious or out of the ordinary from where Ryan was sitting, and when Steph came back into the room with several glasses of iced tea, she looked cool as a cucumber. "So how was last night's wedding? Anything exciting happen?"

It was a perfectly normal question and yet...

Ryan took a sip of his drink and smiled. "Why? What have you heard?"

Steph chuckled. "Me? I haven't heard anything. Why?"

He shrugged. "Just wondering."

"I thought you would have been on your way back home by now. Don't you have work tomorrow?"

"I'll be heading back tonight," he said lightly. "Since I'm the boss, I'm allowed to go in late on Mondays if I want to. Besides, I wanted to take the opportunity to come and see you. You're always telling me I don't do it enough."

Steph smiled warmly at him and then looked over at Tricia. "Did you have a good time last night?"

"Absolutely," Tricia replied. "They had a great menu and the cake was to die for. You would have loved it."

"Well, if one of my kids ever gets married, maybe I'll get the opportunity to try some wedding cake," she said, grinning.

"That's an odd thing to comment on," Ryan said, placing his glass down on the coffee table. "You're not usually one of those moms who harps on when their children are going to get married."

She shrugged. "All this talk about weddings lately just got me thinking. You and your brother aren't getting any younger. It wouldn't kill either of you to get married and maybe give me some grandchildren. It might be nice to..."

The sound of a glass crashing in one of the back rooms brought everyone to their feet.

"I knew it," Ryan said, rushing out of the room ahead of his mother.

"Ryan!" she called out to him. "It's not what you think...if you could just..."

But he wasn't listening. He opened the closed bedroom door and froze.

"Hey, Ryan! What a surprise seeing you here."

It was Sean.

Nine

Without thinking, Tricia ran into the room and into Sean's arms. He was sitting on the bed, his leg elevated on a pillow. "Ohmygod!" she cried. "I can't believe you're really here! Why didn't you tell me you were coming home? When did you get here?" She was rambling and so relieved to see him that it took a minute for the reality of the situation to actually hit. When it did, she pulled back and straightened. "Wait," she said slowly. "You're here."

He nodded, smiling, but his expression turned wary after a minute.

"But…"

Ryan came to stand beside her, his expression one of barely-concealed rage. "How are you feeling?" he asked and Tricia could feel the tension radiating from him.

"I'm uncomfortable," Sean said. "Between the cast on my leg and wrist and my ribs healing, it's hard to find a position that works."

"It must have been a real pain on such a long flight home," Ryan said stiffly.

"I was able to get a first-class seat so I had a little more room, but still…"

"How long have you been here?" Tricia asked, no longer feeling the joy of a few minutes ago.

Confusion was the main emotion at the moment. Sean was home. He hadn't called her and he had been pretending last night while they Skyped that he was still in Japan.

Sean looked beyond Ryan and Trish to his mother. She stepped forward. "A couple of weeks," she said quietly, sitting down at the foot of the bed.

Tricia was just about to yell about the entire situation when Ryan spoke up. "So you've been here all this time, getting a kick out of making Tricia and I look like idiots."

"It wasn't like that, Ryan," Sean began.

"Oh, really? Well then why don't you tell me how it was because from where I'm standing, it seemed like you were having a lot of fun at our expense. Skyping and pretending you were still overseas, making us both keep up this farce at the weddings, I mean…what the hell, Sean?" he yelled.

"Okay, look…in the beginning, I really didn't think I'd be able to come home any time soon. But then I was able to talk with the doctors and got the clearance to travel. And believe me, it was a bitch. I was in pain for every minute of that flight."

"That doesn't explain why you didn't tell us," Tricia snapped, beyond annoyed with her best friend.

Sean sighed. "Look, if I had called and gone to your house, Trish, you would have hovered and skipped out on the weddings. I didn't want you to do that. You and Ryan were having a good time and getting along great and I didn't want to mess with that. Then Mom suggested bringing me here and..." He shrugged. "You know how much I love the beach. It's not a bad way to recuperate."

"Seriously," Ryan said loudly, "what is your damn obsession with these weddings? So what if Tricia didn't go to them? Life would have gone on, Sean! You sat back and played puppet master with the two of us and I want to know why! You know, I have a life back in Jersey! I had better things to do than drive out here all the damn time playing Ken and Barbie at a bunch of parties!"

Tricia gasped as if she had been slapped. She knew Ryan hadn't been thrilled with the prospect of taking Sean's place, but she didn't realize he felt this strongly about it. She thought they'd moved on from that. And while it was completely understandable that he was upset with his brother, she couldn't help but feel hurt by what he was saying.

"Oh for crying out loud," Sean said with frustration. "We all know you have a life, Ryan! Work is all you do! That's your life! So I thought it would be a good thing to force you to get out a little! Sue me!"

Rather than argue, Ryan stormed from the room, but Tricia's eyes never left Sean.

"Come on," Sean said to her, "this isn't that big of a deal, right? I thought it would be a good thing – for the both of you."

"You lied to me," she finally said. "In all the years we've known each other, we never lied to one another."

"It wasn't like that, Trish…"

She felt tears welling in her eyes and then shook her head. "That's exactly what it was. Do you have any idea how worried I've been about you? Do you know how awkward it was to go to the weddings with Ryan instead of you? Did it even occur once to you to talk to me about this crazy plan of yours?"

Steph stood and took one of Tricia's hands in hers. "It isn't all Sean's fault," she said shyly. "I…I sort of had a hand in it too."

"What?" Tricia pulled her hand away, dismay written all over her face as she looked between mother and son. "Why?"

Sighing, Steph seemed to sag with defeat. "The very first time I met you, I knew you were someone special. I saw the connection between you and Sean and it used to make me so happy to see the two of you together. But I knew after a while, the two of you would never be anything more than friends." She looked up at Tricia. "Not that it's a bad thing…"

"I need to go…" Tricia said and turned to leave.

"Don't go, Trish," Sean called out. "Just…just wait."

She sighed but kept looking over her shoulder for Ryan. For all she knew, he was on the ferry back to town without her.

"You are the daughter I never had," Steph finally said after a minute. "You're already part of the family and for years I have been racking my brain to find a way to fix you and Ryan up. So when this opportunity presented itself," she said with a shrug, "I kind of took advantage of it."

Anger and frustration warred within her. She glared at Sean. "Are you even really hurt or was this all part of your plan?"

He looked hurt by her words. "I would never lie…" And then he stopped himself.

"Exactly," Tricia said with disgust and left the room. She didn't stop until she was out in the front yard, and that's where she found Ryan. She stopped beside him. "Are you all right?"

He shook his head. "I want to go back in there and throttle him, but I can't! I mean, what the hell was he thinking?"

She shared with him what Steph had just told her and then watched as it just seemed to spur his anger on.

"Are you kidding me? So…what…we were some sort of social experiment?" He looked beyond Tricia toward the house. "They came up with this stupid plan and were just sitting back, being entertained while watching us?" His gaze came back to hers. "Doesn't it make you mad?"

"It does!" she cried. "But…I can understand – sort of – why they did it. And…it didn't turn out all that bad, right?" She placed a hand on his arm and gently squeezed. "I'll admit I don't like the idea of being the last to know but I'm really glad we got to know each other. This last month has been wonderful. I...I thought you felt the same way."

He raked a hand through his hair in frustration. "That's not the point! They manipulated us and...and...is Sean even hurt?" Growling with frustration, he turned away from her and began to pace. "I was so damn worried about him. Was it all for nothing?"

"I asked him the same thing and he claims that part is true. Everything else just sort of fell into place."

"This is unbelievable," he muttered.

For a minute, Tricia thought he was going to go back into the house and confront his family, but he didn't. With one last look of disgust at the house, he began to walk away. "I'm heading back to the ferry."

She wasn't sure what she was supposed to do. Part of her wanted to go back inside and hash things out with Sean. In all their years of friendship, they'd never walked away from an argument, never stayed mad. But the need to go with Ryan and make sure they were okay was stronger. Helplessly, she looked back at the house before taking off after Ryan.

They didn't speak the entire way home. Tricia was even afraid that Ryan was simply going to drop her off and leave. Then she remembered he still had his luggage in the house and sighed with relief knowing she still had a few more minutes to figure out what to say.

When he stormed into the house and up to the bedroom, she followed. At the sight of him throwing his things together, she finally snapped.

"Hey!"

Ryan looked up at her, his expression angry, but he didn't speak.

"What are you doing?"

"What does it look like?" he asked, tossing item after item back into his bag.

"Why are you mad at me over this? I was just as much in the dark as you were!"

He straightened and looked at her with disbelief. "I'm finding that a little hard to believe."

"Excuse me?" she asked incredulously. "Where the hell did that even come from?"

He sighed loudly with frustration. "You and my brother are closer than any people I know. You tell each other everything! You can't honestly expect me to stand here and believe that he didn't tell you any of this?"

"That's exactly what I'm telling you!"

"And yet I still don't believe it," he said and went back to his packing.

Reaching over, Tricia pulled the duffle bag away and tossed it across the room and for a minute, felt a bit of shock at her behavior. "After everything we've shared this last month, you can stand here and think I lied to you?" He didn't say a word. He didn't have to. His expression said it all. And then the devastation of that hit her. Tears welled in her eyes and she quickly turned away so he wouldn't see them. "Yeah, so…if that's what you believe, then you really should go."

She walked out of the room and down the stairs. By the time she was outside on the back deck, the tears flowed freely. How could he possibly believe that she'd lie to him? Adding to that misery was the fact that Sean had lied to her. How did it all go so wrong so fast? In a few hours she'd managed to lose all the people who mattered most to her.

Looking at the fish in the pond, she sat down on the deck. In the back of her mind she really believed Ryan was going to realize he was wrong and come down to talk to her.

But he didn't.

In the distance she heard his car door slam and then the engine start. It didn't take a genius to know he was leaving.

Without even saying goodbye.

Bastard. That was it? After everything they had shared, he was able to simply pack up and leave without a word? She wasn't sure if she should scream with rage or continue to cry with heartache.

She did both.

It took a while but when she finally pulled herself together, she was completely spent. It was hard to figure out what it was she was crying for most. Ryan leaving without saying goodbye? The fact he thought she'd lied to him? Or being lied to by Sean? The answer wasn't clear and Tricia knew it would be a while before it actually was.

"Mental health day," she muttered as she walked back into the house. When she found her purse, she pulled out her phone, hit a couple of screens to turn off her voicemail and shut it off. She was one of the few people who still also had a house phone and she went and unplugged it too. Walking around, she closed the French doors and locked them before doing the same to the front door – and bolting it – before closing all the blinds.

For now, she just wanted to make the world go away.

****

Ryan drove as if he were trying to escape something.

And in his own mind, he was.

Maybe he was overreacting, or maybe he was starting to get a little spooked by how fast he had fallen for Tricia and subconsciously needed an excuse to walk away.

"Bullshit," he murmured. Ryan knew he wasn't a coward even though his current actions said otherwise. So his mother and brother set him up? Was it really such a bad thing? It wasn't as if they'd set him up with a stranger or with the date from hell; it was Tricia. He'd always liked her, so why was he so upset?

Because they made you look like a fool.

Did they? Thinking back over the last six weeks, Ryan realized that every minute he had spent with Tricia, he'd enjoyed. And other than his worry over Sean and his accident, things had been good. Really good.

And then he went and screwed them up.

Did Sean tell Tricia what he was doing? Wracking his brain he couldn't find any trace or memory of anything she said or did that would prove that. She was a sweet and honest person and from everything he ever knew about her, she certainly wasn't a manipulator. If anything, Ryan knew people tended to take advantage of her because she was too nice. He didn't think she would have gone along with this plan even if she'd had a crush on him long before now.

His heart ached with the memory of the look on her face when they'd gotten back to the house. How the hell was he supposed to make it up to her? The last thing he wanted to do was be one of those people who took advantage of her kindness.

He was clueless as to how to get out of this. Sure there was begging and groveling, but…being who Tricia was, she'd forgive him even if she was still hurting. He cursed himself and his short temper. He was angry with his mother and brother, not Tricia. She'd just been the closest one when he unloaded. A convenient punching bag.

And that made him loathe himself even more.

A look at the dashboard clock showed he had another hour on the road before he got home. The only decision he could make was to give Tricia a little space.

He'd deal with his family first.

****

By Tuesday, Ryan was ready to climb the walls. Thirteen times he'd called Tricia. *Thirteen!* No answer, no answering machine and no voicemail. What the hell was she doing? In his frustration, he punched the kitchen wall and cursed. He knew she was upset but he didn't expect a complete shutout like this. How the hell was he supposed to apologize when she wouldn't answer her phone?

He collapsed on his sofa, ran his hands over his face and sighed with frustration. Sunday morning, he thought he had it all – Tricia in his arms, a beautiful day outside and thoughts of a future together that weren't overly freaking him out. And now where was he? Alone, pissed off and everything looked like shit.

Coward.

Yeah, that pretty much was the only way to describe himself. After talking for hours with his mother and brother, he knew now what they did was truly done out of love. His mother was a bit scary in her ability to know when people were meant to be together and he knew how much she believed in the connection he and Tricia had.

Had.

Hard to tell if there was still a connection when she wouldn't talk to him. The thought of jumping in the car and going to her was appealing but it was also impossible. His work schedule was jam-packed and even now he was running late for a meeting because he was sitting here obsessing about the whole situation.

With nothing left to do, he got himself ready and out the door. He owned a company and he had work to do and as much as it pained him, he'd have to wait to take that drive until Friday.

****

You know, you can take a dozen showers, wash the sheets and put all the little mementos away, but there was no way to cleanse your heart and mind, Tricia thought to herself as she walked in the door after work late Tuesday afternoon.

She used to love coming home to this house, but now it just made her sad. All the things she'd loved about it – her connection to the Petersons – were just more reasons to make her heart ache.

In the kitchen she glanced in the refrigerator for inspiration for dinner and then glanced over at the unplugged phone. For days she'd managed to turn off the voicemail on her cell phone but knew that wouldn't last much longer. Her clients needed a way to get in touch with her and it really was childish to keep avoiding everyone. She hadn't done anything wrong so really, it was time to be a big girl and deal with reality.

As soon as the plug was back in, her phone rang and she let the answering machine pick up.

She'd deal with being a big girl later.

"Tricia? Are you there?" Ryan's voice filled the room. "I've been calling all day. Well, for several days and…I um…look, I'm at home so please call me when you get this, okay?" He paused. "Please." And then he hung up.

Her heart was hammering so fiercely in her chest she almost had herself convinced she was having a heart attack. After a few deep breaths, things went back to normal. The fact was she wasn't ready to talk to him yet. She needed more time.

In an attempt to distract herself, she went back to the refrigerator to find something to eat, but her eyes kept going back to the damn blinking light on the answering machine. "I can't deal with this right now," she muttered, grabbing her purse and walking out of the kitchen. "I prefer takeout anyway."

****

When Tricia pulled into her driveway Friday evening, she saw a car parked there and recognized it immediately as Steph's. She supposed out of the three Petersons, she was feeling the most kindly toward her. And for the first time since Tricia had moved in, Steph was waiting outside rather than using her key.

"Hey," Tricia said cautiously as she climbed from her car. "What are you doing here?"

"I figured it might be best if I showed up unannounced, especially after the way things went last weekend." She looked contrite and smiled weakly. "May I come in?"

"Of course."

Once inside, Tricia realized she wasn't angry anymore, not really. So Steph and Sean had set her up with Ryan. What was the big deal? Sure, she would have preferred it if they had talked to her about it first but in the long run, she had really enjoyed herself, had loved getting to know him. It wasn't their fault he turned out to be a big jerk.

"So what brings you here, Steph?" Placing her purse down on the living room sofa, she sat and waited.

"I hate the way we left things on Sunday, Trish. You have to know we did this with the best of intentions. Ryan's not overly social and you tend to be shy and when Sean had his accident and he told me about the weddings, well…I just sort of planted the idea with him to set the two of you up." She shook her head. "That didn't come out right, what I meant is…"

"I know what you meant," Tricia said softly, "and believe it or not, I'm glad you did."

"You are?"

Tricia nodded. "I'm more upset that you didn't talk to me first." She shrugged. "I really enjoyed the time Ryan and I spent together."

"But...?" Steph prompted.

"But...it's over now."

"What? Why?"

Tricia told her about the argument they'd had before he left. "The thing is, I really thought we had something serious. I...I was falling in love with him and the fact that he would accuse me of lying to him? Well...it just showed me we weren't on the same page."

"I see." They sat in silence for a few minutes. "Do you miss him?"

Tricia nodded and willed herself not to cry. She had managed to go for all of sixteen hours without crying over the last week.

"Why don't you call him? It seems to me like things just got out of hand and I take full responsibility for it. I talked to him on Sunday when he was driving home and I thought we were all good, but apparently not. He said he was going to call you..."

"He did," Tricia said quietly. "I just haven't answered any of his calls."

"Ah…and how's that working for you?"

Tricia couldn't help but chuckle. Steph was never one for beating around the bush.

"Honestly? It's not. But I know my own strengths and weaknesses and I know if I talk to him right now, he'll convince me of how sorry he is. And I'm sure he is but…he really hurt me, Steph. I pride myself on being the type of person people can trust and the fact that he didn't?" She sighed. "I…I just need some time."

Steph took one of her hands in hers and squeezed. "Then you should take it."

"I'm just not sure when it stops being what I need and starts being cowardly."

"Only you can answer that." Steph rose and went to the kitchen to pour them each something to drink. When she came back and handed Tricia the glass, she smiled. "Why don't you come over to the island for the weekend and hang out with Sean? I have plans with some friends up in Vermont but I hate leaving him alone."

"Vermont? That's kind of a long haul for you, isn't it?"

She nodded. "I know. And I almost canceled because I need to be there for Sean, but he insisted I go. He said he was tired of people fussing over him."

"How is he feeling?"

"He's getting along pretty well with the crutches – even with the small cast on his arm – but I don't let him do too much. I know he'd love to see you."

Part of her really wanted to see him too, but not yet, which is what she told Steph. "Actually, I was planning on going upstate to visit my mom and John this weekend. I'm sorry."

"You don't owe me an apology, sweetheart. I just thought it might work out and it would be a good time for you and Sean to have some uninterrupted time to sort things out." She bent down and kissed the top of Tricia's head. "When are you hitting the road for your mom's?"

"Early tomorrow morning. It's a three-hour drive – give or take – and if I leave early we'll have the whole day together."

"So you're only going for the day?"

Tricia shook her head. "The weekend. Maybe more. I don't have any clients until Tuesday but I was waiting to see how the weekend went before deciding when to come home."

"Then how about you and I go and grab a bite to eat? It's been a long time since we've gone out just the two of us."

It was true and as much as Tricia wanted to bow out so she could pack and relax and continue to wallow in self-pity as she'd been doing for a week, she knew she needed to get out of the house and move on.

Ryan hadn't tried to call her in a couple of days and she figured he'd finally given up. It was for the best. They'd tried something and it didn't work. Not every relationship led to love, marriage and happily-ever-after.

No matter how much you wanted it.

"Tricia?" Steph prompted.

"What? Oh, dinner, right? Sure! That sounds great." She stood and reached for her purse. "There's a new Mexican place in town I know you're going to love."

Ten

It was after dark Sunday night and Ryan was sitting on the front steps of Tricia's house with his head resting in his hands. It would have been easier to go inside, but he felt he no longer had the right to do that. So he waited.

When he'd arrived Saturday morning, he'd cursed himself when he saw she wasn't home. His plan had been to arrive on Friday night like they always did but after his meeting with a difficult client went well into the night, he knew he needed to get a good night's sleep before hitting the road.

He'd called his mother to see if she knew where Tricia was, but she didn't. He wasn't quite sure he believed her, but at the time, he didn't have a choice. She herself was on her way to Vermont to visit some friends. Then he'd called Sean and talked to him for a while and he claimed he hadn't seen or talked to Tricia since the previous weekend. With nothing to do but wait, Ryan had reluctantly agreed to take the ferry over to Fire Island to stay with his brother. It wasn't ideal and it wouldn't help him to know when Tricia would be home but again, he didn't have much of a choice.

So here he sat. Waiting.

Looking at his watch he figured he'd give it another hour and then he'd have to head home. It was hard to believe she still wasn't home and no one knew where she went. Worry for her nearly overwhelmed him and when he spotted headlights at the end of the block, he said a silent prayer it was her.

The car came to a stop a few feet away from him and Ryan instantly stood. He could see the frown on Tricia's face and hated he was the reason for it. With his hands in his pockets, he watched as she climbed from the car, grocery bags in her hands. When he stepped forward to help her, she merely moved around him.

"Hey," he said quietly. "How are you?"

If she heard him, she didn't let on. Unlocking the door, she moved into the house and put the bags down in the kitchen before turning around and going back out to the car. Ryan followed and watched as she opened the trunk and pulled out a small suitcase.

"Where've you been?" he asked.

Still no answer.

Then she reached back into the car for what looked like a bag from the local Chinese restaurant. If he had to guess, he'd say she was away for the weekend and stopped to pick up dinner on her way home. But where had she gone and was she going to acknowledge him?

Without asking, he took the suitcase from her hands and walked back into the house, placing it on the stairs before following her into the kitchen. She was getting a plate and silverware and acting as if he wasn't even there.

"Okay, I get it. You're still mad," he said finally. "But I'm here and I've been here all weekend because I think we need to talk."

Tricia slammed her fork down and looked at him. "Oh, *now* you feel like we need to talk? Because I thought we needed to do that a week ago. But you know what happened? You left." She never raised her voice but the irritation was definitely there.

"I know I handled things poorly and I'm sorry. I tried to apologize but you wouldn't take my calls. Then I came here and you weren't here. Where were you?"

She looked at him incredulously for a minute and then went back to plating her dinner. "I'm sorry you drove all the way out here for nothing. It's late, I've been gone all weekend and I have things to do. Besides, you have a long drive ahead of you so you should get going."

He sighed with frustration and moved to stand in front of her. "I'm not going anywhere until we talk."

She stepped away from him and took a seat at the breakfast nook. "Fine. Clearly you have something to say, so go ahead."

Ryan wasn't stupid. Tricia wasn't even trying to hide her animosity toward him so he knew he had his work cut out for him. "I screwed up," he began. "Seeing Sean at my mom's after he'd been a jerk on Skype at the wedding, it messed with me a little. It pissed me off that he was home and he kept it from me. While I'll admit Sean and I aren't as close as the two of you are, he's never deliberately lied to me."

"Me either," she said quietly.

"By the time I was getting my brain wrapped around all of it, you came out and said how it was all a set up. I didn't think. I just reacted and I'm sorry." His expression softened as he looked at her. He'd missed her so damn much and now that he was here, all he wanted to do was hold her, kiss her, love her.

"I really am sorry, sweetheart," he said, slowly walking over to her. "I know you had no idea what the two of them were doing and I never should have accused you of it."

"No, you shouldn't have."

When he was close enough to touch her, he did. His fingers skimmed down her cheek and he felt like everything was going to be all right. "Tell me you forgive me," he said, his voice rough like gravel. "I need to know we're okay."

Tricia took a shaky breath and met his gaze. "I know it was a sucky situation and I can understand you reacting badly. I don't agree with it, but yes. I forgive you."

He almost sagged with relief. Leaning in, he went to kiss her when her hand on his chest stopped him.

"But…"

And that's when he knew he was in trouble. "But...?"

"We're not okay, Ryan," she said softly. "You've known me almost as long as Sean has and although we weren't close until recently, you should have known I wasn't involved in any of it. And yet you still accused me." She shrugged. "You didn't trust me and you didn't even respect me enough to let me defend myself. I've been in relationships like this before and I can't do it again. I'm sorry."

Ryan felt as if he couldn't breathe.

He'd ruined it.

He'd finally found the woman he wanted to spend the rest of his life with and he screwed it up.

"Trish," he whispered. "Please."

The sound of the house phone ringing stopped any response she may have had. Ryan wasn't sure if he was grateful or not. He stepped aside as she stood and walked around him to get to the phone.

He raked a hand through his hair and tried to regroup. How was he going to convince Tricia to give him another chance? What could he possibly do or say to...

"Ryan?" she said, her expression wary. "It's for you." She held the phone out to him.

"Who is it?"

"It's some doctor calling from up in Vermont. Your mom's in the hospital."

****

If Tricia wasn't in the middle of it, she'd swear it was a bad joke.

It was after eleven by the time they got on the road. Ryan had spent a long time on the phone with the doctor and then had to call Sean. They had debated on whether or not he should go to Vermont with Ryan, but in the end decided against it. Not because of his injuries, but because it would be too hard for him to get the ferry.

In the end, Tricia insisted on going with him. While Ryan had been sorting things out with Sean, Tricia had gone online to find them a hotel near the hospital. With the reservations made, all she had to do was pack and they were ready to go.

Ryan insisted on driving and she could see how tense he was. She wished there was something she could do or say to help him.

"She's going to be fine, Ryan," she said softly when they hit the expressway. "You know your mom is stronger than both of us together. What did the doctor say?"

He shrugged. "They believe she had a heart attack," he said wearily. "I can't even process it. She's too young for something like that." He shook his head. "At least, in my mind she's too young."

"Could it be something else?"

"I have no idea and being that they hadn't finished any tests, it's anyone's guess."

Reaching over, she placed her hand on his leg, simply needing to touch him. Without taking his eyes from the road, he placed his hand on top of hers. They drove like that the remainder of the time.

Tricia had dozed off at some point and woke up as they pulled up to their hotel. It was more of a bed and breakfast, but it was the only place where she could find a room on short notice. While Ryan handled the luggage, she went inside and took care of checking them in, apologizing to the innkeeper for the late check-in.

"We have a reservation for Peterson," she said with a smile.

"Ah, yes," the woman at the desk said pleasantly. It was not a high-tech establishment and Tricia couldn't help but smile when she was handed an old-fashioned key for their room. "You're in room number four. Second floor, last door on your left." She pointed toward the large staircase.

With a word of thanks, she turned toward the stairs. It was an old Victorian house and at any other time, she would have loved to explore it and learn about its history, but tonight wasn't the time. She looked over her shoulder and saw Ryan walking toward her. He looked exhausted and she knew more than anything, he needed to get some rest.

At the room, Tricia opened the door, a small gasp of delight escaped when she caught a glimpse of the interior. It normally wasn't her style, but the massive canopied four-poster bed was beautiful. The room was large and airy but the décor was definitely in theme with the house. There were fresh flowers on the dresser and a fruit basket on the small table by a bay window.

"There weren't any normal hotels available?" Ryan asked as he put their luggage down.

"None that were close to the hospital. I thought this was better."

He made a non-committal sound and walked around the room. "I'm going to call the hospital and see if they have any news on Mom."

"It's three in the morning, Ryan," she said. "Why don't we grab a couple of hours sleep and just plan on getting there early? I don't want you to be disappointed if they don't let you talk to anyone."

She knew he wanted to argue, but exhaustion won out. "I guess," he mumbled and kicked his shoes off.

Grabbing her bag, Tricia went into the bathroom to change. It seemed silly – it wasn't as if he hadn't seen her naked multiple times – but that was before. When she stepped out five minutes later, Ryan was down to his briefs and pulling the quilt down on the bed. They climbed into the massive bed on opposite sides, but when he reached for her, she went willingly.

He didn't say a word. All he did was hold her and she felt extremely content with the feel of his strong arms around her. Snuggling deeper into his embrace, she sighed and fell asleep.

****

They were at the hospital by nine in the morning. Tricia had gone and grabbed them coffee from the cafeteria while Ryan sat and waited to talk to Steph's doctor. She met up with them on a sofa in the lobby and silently handed Ryan his cup, careful not to interrupt the conversation.

"Basically, Mr. Peterson, your mother is very lucky. Her friends acted quickly and she received the attention she needed at the right time," the doctor said.

Tricia saw Ryan visibly sag with relief before asking, "So was it a heart attack?"

The doctor shook his head. "Anxiety. They can present the same and I'm glad we had the opportunity to verify that. We'll be releasing her after lunch."

"Wait, wait, wait…anxiety? How is that even possible? My mother is the mellowest person I've ever met!"

The doctor stood and smiled. "You'll have to talk to her about that." He looked at his watch. "Visiting hours will start up in about forty-five minutes. You can see her then." He shook both their hands before turning and walking away.

Ryan seemed in shock. "An anxiety attack? Seriously?" He looked over at Tricia. "He's kidding, right?"

"I don't think so. He seemed pretty serious about it. Thank God it wasn't anything worse."

"I just don't understand how it's possible. You know my mom. Nothing bothers her. She does all that yoga crap and is always on us about how we all need to go with the flow and relax. What the hell does she have anxiety over?"

She reached over and squeezed his hand. "We're going to have to wait to find out."

****

"Oh, the two of you came together!" Steph said with delight when they walked through the hospital room door. "I'm so pleased!"

Ryan felt instantly tense and had a sense of déjà vu. He was beginning to hate the fact that he doubted any of his family's illnesses and had to wonder if Steph had really had an anxiety attack or if this her way of getting him and Tricia together.

Well, the joke was on her, since Tricia didn't seem to want anything to do with him. Okay, maybe that wasn't completely true. She had slept in his arms all night and if it wasn't for the fact that he was completely exhausted, he might have tried to seduce her.

All in good time.

"I happened to be at Tricia's when we got the call. The doctor called Tricia's house looking for me rather than my cell phone. Care to tell me how that happened?" he asked with more than a hint of suspicion.

"You called and told me you were looking for her, Ryan. I didn't need to do any great detective work. And I know Tricia's home phone number by heart. Your cell phone number is programmed into my phone so I don't even have to look at it."

Tricia knew it made sense but being that they were just getting over a similar deception, she could understand Ryan's unease. Before he could argue with her further, Tricia spoke up. "How are you feeling?"

Steph waved a hand at her. "I'm embarrassed more than anything." She rolled her eyes. "Anxiety! I still can't believe it. When I think about the pain and how I felt last night, I honestly would have sworn I was having a heart attack!"

"What caused it, Mom?" Before she could answer, there was a knock on the door and an older gentleman walked in. Tricia and Ryan looked at the man, then at Steph. "Mom?"

"Oh…um…Paul, this is my son Ryan and this is Tricia." She looked at the two of them. "This is my friend Paul."

They all shook hands and Tricia had a feeling things were only going to get worse before they got better. "So…Steph, you were about to tell us what happened when you had the anxiety attack."

Paul looked at Steph and smiled. "I'm glad that's all it was." He took her hand in his and then kissed it.

Beside her, Tricia could feel the tension radiating off of Ryan. "Mom?" he prompted one more time.

Steph sighed. "Okay, fine. Paul and I have been seeing each other for quite some time. We came up here to get away for a little bit." She looked sheepish. "I love your brother and I know I promised to take care of him but he's exhausting! I just needed a little time away. So when Paul suggested a quick trip, I readily agreed."

"So are you worrying about Sean?" Tricia asked.

"No," Steph said and then looked up at Paul. "Last night, Paul asked me to marry him and...well...that's when I had the anxiety attack."

"Oh my..." Tricia said and nervously glanced at Ryan.

"Growing up," he began, "you always told me and Sean that there wasn't anything we couldn't say to you. No secrets. No lying. And it seems to me that's all you've been doing for the last couple of weeks." There was no anger; only disappointment laced his words. "I don't know why you felt the need to keep this a secret. Sean and I knew you dated, Mom. It would have been nice if you would have found a less dramatic way to introduce us all."

She nodded. "You're right. I guess I had hoped that my boys would settle down and then I'd allow myself the opportunity to do the same. Your dad's been gone for a long time and for so long, my whole focus has been on you and Sean."

"Is that why you were so anxious to set me and Tricia up?" Ryan asked.

Shaking her head, Steph smiled. "Sweetheart, I've been wanting to do that for years. And it had nothing to do with me and everything to do with the fact that the two of you are perfect for each other."

Tricia felt herself blushing from head to toe.

"So…what now?" Ryan asked. "The two of you have been dating, he's proposed, and I know your night was interrupted, but did you give him an answer?"

Now Steph blushed. "Actually, we decided to wait a little while – for all the reasons you mentioned. I haven't let him meet you and Sean – and Tricia – and it's important to us that everyone get to know each other."

Ryan smiled and walked closer to the bed and kissed his mother on the cheek. "I think that's a great idea." He straightened and looked at Paul. "So…tell me about yourself."

****

They stayed at the hospital with Steph until the doctors released her. To Tricia's surprise, Ryan didn't argue when Steph said she was going home with Paul and that she'd be in touch. As a matter of fact, he almost seemed happy about it. She waited until they were back in their room at the inn before asking him about it.

He sighed lightly. "I've been waiting for the time when my mom would settle down again. She's been on the go for years with traveling and visiting friends and even though I don't know anything about Paul other than what he just told us back at the hospital, my mother is an excellent judge of character. If he makes her happy, then I'm happy."

"Alrighty then," Tricia said with a smile. "I'm glad you're okay with the whole thing."

"And I know she's serious about him if his proposal gave her an anxiety attack. Nothing rattles my mom so if Paul did, then I'd say it's even more of a good thing." He walked over to the window and looked out at the property before turning back toward her. "I'm going to give Sean a call with the update. I didn't want to do it while we were there."

"Okay."

"Unless…you want to call him?"

She knew what he was doing. By now he had to know she hadn't spoken to Sean in over a week and he was giving her the opening she needed to take that first step. But she wasn't ready.

"That's okay. You can do it." Relief swamped her when he didn't argue. She took the time to go around and pack up her things. Now that they knew Steph was all right, they would probably get back on the road for home. Knowing Ryan, he had a ton of work waiting for him and Tricia knew he hated when his schedule got disrupted, even if it was for a good reason.

When he got off the phone and saw her bags by the door, he looked at her quizzically. "What's going on?"

She looked at the door and back at him. "I…I just figured we'd be heading back. Steph's okay and she's staying with Paul for a few days, so there's nothing left for us to do." She shrugged. "I would think you'd be anxious to get home and back to work."

"I took a couple of extra days off," he said mildly, watching her carefully. "What about you? Do you have clients you're missing today?"

"No. I actually don't have any until Wednesday."

"So why the rush?"

"Ryan," she sighed. "There's no reason to stay."

Slowly he walked over to her and placed his hands on her shoulders. "I disagree," he said softly. "I think it might be nice for us to stay another night." Carefully, he pulled her in closer. "We could walk around the grounds outside, do a little sightseeing, have dinner…"

It sounded wonderful to her, but Tricia couldn't help but be cautious. "I don't know…"

"I'm not ready to give up on us, Tricia. I know I hurt you and I want to prove to you that I'm the right man for you. Please."

"But…what about…"

He placed a finger over her lips. "I was wrong." Leaning forward, he rested his forehead against hers. "I'm not perfect, Tricia, and there are going to be times when I say or do something stupid. I can't help it."

She gave him a weak smile. "I will too."

"I didn't expect this," he said softly. "I didn't expect you. But I'm not sorry for it. We may have known each other for years but the time wasn't right for us until now." His expression turned serious as he lifted his head and looked at her. "I love you."

A soft gasp escaped her lips as her eyes went wide.

"It's true," he said. "This all took me completely by surprise and I didn't want to believe it at first. I couldn't believe we would be the ones to be together. I always looked at you like you were Sean's girl."

Tricia shook her head. "It was never like that for us. We were friends. He's my best friend and I love him but there's never been anything romantic between us."

"I didn't believe that for a long time. Even after we started seeing each other, I still kept thinking in the back of my mind that if it were Sean there, you would choose him."

"It was never a competition. Sean's my friend, but it's you I'm in love with."

A slow smile crossed his lips. "Is it?"

She nodded.

"Say it," he whispered.

"I love you, Ryan Peterson. You and no one else."

Wrapping her in his arms, he kissed her. And kept on kissing her until she agreed to stay with him not only for another night in Vermont, but for the rest of their lives.

Epilogue

Ten months later…

"You have *got* to be kidding me!"

Tricia chuckled as she sat back on her deck looking at Sean. He had just walked through the French doors, his hands full of what looked to be the mail. "Problem?"

"I thought we were through with all of this stuff last summer. And now…"

"Well, to be fair, you didn't have to go through anything last summer. You were laid up with your casts and missed all the fun. We're all just making sure you get the full experience this time around."

All around her, everyone chucked – Ryan, Steph and Paul.

"Yeah, well…you guys suck. How am I supposed to deal with all of this?" Sean cried, taking a seat on the bench overlooking the pond.

"We were very considerate of your schedule," Ryan began with a grin, his arm wrapped around Tricia's shoulders. "You said you were home until the middle of August so we made sure we stayed in that time frame."

Sean snorted with disgust. "The only reason there's a time frame is because you're sending me to do those job bids out in California!" Since his recovery, Sean had finally taken his brother up on his offer to go into business together.

"You said you didn't mind the traveling," Ryan reminded. "And I know how you hate to be still for too long. We're merely providing some things for you to do."

"There's two engagement parties, two wedding showers and two weddings! We've got something going on practically every weekend for the entire summer. When am I supposed to have any time to myself?" Sean said with exasperation.

"If you'd like, we can find someone to help you," Steph said, grinning too. "Like a partner to help you plan all these events."

"Plan?! I thought I was just a guest!"

"You're my best man," Ryan said. "You'll need to organize and plan my bachelor party and…"

"No strippers!" Tricia interrupted.

Ryan kissed her on the cheek. "With no strippers, of course. And being that the wedding shower is co-ed, you'll have to help plan what the guys are doing."

"Oh, for the love of it…"

"And since you and Ryan are my sons, I'll expect you to take care of some of the details for mine and Paul's wedding," Steph added. "You more so than

Ryan since he'll be busy with his own wedding plans."

"Are you people for real?" Sean asked wearily. "Couldn't you space this out any better?"

"You're a flight risk – or you have the potential to be," Ryan reminded him. "We wanted to make sure you were here for all of the festivities."

"Trish, come on. Be on my side," Sean begged. "Help me out."

She laughed. "Sorry, buddy. I had to give up having you as my maid of honor since you're going to be Ryan's best man. The most I can do is hook you up with my cousin Angie to help you out with some of it."

"Angie? I don't even know who that is!"

"You never met her. She's my cousin on my dad's side. We hadn't seen each other in years and we reconnected not too long ago. It turns out she has a real knack for party planning. She's cute," she teased. "You'll like her."

"Great," Sean mumbled.

"Who knows," Ryan said with a laugh. "Maybe she can be your date for this year's wedding season!"

Sean shot to his feet with his hands in the air in frustration. "You know what? Make fun all you want but I don't need any help or any dates. So keep your matchmaking and planning to yourselves. I can do it on my own just fine!" He walked back into Tricia's house and slammed the door.

"Poor boy," Steph said but didn't sound the least bit sorry.

"Little does he know that working with Angie wasn't a suggestion," Tricia said with a wicked grin.

Ryan nodded, pulling her close. "It's kind of nice knowing that this time we'll be the ones sitting back and watching all the fun."

They all laughed at the inside joke.

Paul joined in the laughter and then looked at the three of them. "I think I'm going to really enjoy being part of this family."

Read an excerpt of
FRIDAY NIGHT
BRIDES

Available Now!

Ten years ago…

"I totally felt like a princess tonight."

"Me too!"

"Is it wrong that I didn't want to put my street clothes back on?"

Hailey James shook her head and laughed. She still couldn't understand what the big deal was. Or maybe she could. The first time in a wedding gown is always a big deal. Well…at least that's what she'd learned after going to work with her mom every weekend at her bridal boutique, Enchanted Bridal, since she was five years old. Maybe she had just become desensitized to it all.

Nah.

Sitting at a table with her three best friends at their favorite café at eleven on a Friday night was the perfect way to cap off the night. Hailey shook her head and smiled as her friends continued to gush about how exciting the night had been.

Every Friday night, Enchanted Bridal held a fashion show—sometimes they were big events at convention centers or hotels, and other times they were scaled back and small and held at the boutique itself. Tonight's was at the boutique and it was the first time in the thirteen years Hailey and her friends had been modeling in the show that her mother let them be brides. They'd started out as flower girl models when they were five so maybe she just figured it was time.

Maybe it was a big deal, she thought. After all, modeling wedding gowns rather than bridesmaid dresses made them the focus of the entire show. As much as Hailey hated to admit it, it had been kind of cool. Even though she'd been playing dress-up in some of those wedding gowns for years, it was completely different when you walked out onto a stage—with a super-hot guy pretending to be your groom—and having everyone's eyes on you.

Okay, yeah, it was exciting.

Hailey sighed. Every weekend she helped brides pick out their dresses and listened to them talk about how happy and in love they were and how wonderful their futures were going to be. It wasn't that she doubted the sentiment, but personally, she had never experienced those overwhelming feelings. And while putting on a dress that made you feel beautiful—like a princess—was great, what Hailey really wanted was to meet a guy who would make her feel like that.

And if it could possibly be one of the many hot models her mother always seemed to find each season, even better. Seriously, her mother had a knack for finding the most amazing looking men. Tonight Hailey had walked with Terrance Adams. He was twenty-three and completely hot. He'd been very nice to her but she got the impression that he looked at her like she was just a kid. So while he was nice to look at, he wasn't going to be her Prince Charming.

But she had no doubt these Friday night shows were going to be the key to finding a hot groom of her own and her ultimate happily ever after.

Resting her cheek in her hand, she laughed as Angie bragged about how great her boobs had looked in her dress tonight. Hailey would never consider talking about her boobs in public, but Angie had no filter. The four of them around this table were as different as night and day and yet…they clicked. It had been that way ever since the first day of kindergarten.

Angie was the loud one.

Becca was the shy one.

Ella was the sweet one.

And Hailey? Well, she was the sensible one. And sensible, she realized, was really just another word for boring or uptight.

Either way, it worked for them.

"You know what I think?" Becca asked them. "I think this is the start of something big for all of us. I think tonight marks our own journey toward getting to wear one of those gowns for real."

"Ugh…" Angie moaned. "We're only eighteen. Do we need to start thinking about our own weddings? Can't we just get through prom? That's causing me enough grief."

"Stop being so cynical. There's nothing wrong with thinking about or just pretending that we know what our future is going to be like," Becca admonished. "So…who's going to go first? Where do you see yourself in say…ten years?"

Even though she thought it was ridiculous, Hailey was the first to play along.

"Me," she said. "In ten years, I imagine myself being madly in love with one of those hot male models Mom always has in the show. They're perfect—and look great in a tux!"

They all laughed. "Way to be superficial," Angie teased.

Hailey shrugged. "I can't help it if I want a man who looks good."

"Me next!" Ella said excitedly. "In ten years I know I'm going to be married to Dylan. We're going to have the perfect, small and intimate wedding I've always wanted with just you guys and a handful of family with us." She sighed happily. "I can't wait!"

"Ten years?" Becca said with disbelief. "You've been dating for years already. Why wait that long?"

Ella shrugged. "Well, hopefully we'll be married by then but we really want to be financially set before we get married."

"So practical," Angie sighed. "What about you, Becs?"

"All I want is to have my own little café and be married to a man who treats me like a princess," she said dreamily. "I've heard there are guys out there who do that—treat girls like that. I just wish I could find one."

"Yikes. You're only eighteen, you know. Give it some time," Angie said. "You all are acting like you need a man to make you happy! You don't!"

"Really? So where do you see yourself in ten years?" Ella challenged.

"I'm going to grab the world by the balls and do whatever it is I want to do because I don't need a man to define me," she challenged.

Everyone went silent.

"Until some guy comes and sweeps you off your feet when you least expect it," Ella said and then giggled. "It's going to be the most fun to prove that you're no different than the rest of us."

"Bring it, bitches," Angie said with a grin.

One

"Seriously, babe. What were you thinking?"

For a minute, Becca could only stare. Was he joking? Had he been paying attention at all? "I...I thought you'd want to come and see the show. That's why we agreed to meet here," she said slowly. Unfortunately, she wasn't sure who she was trying to explain it to—Danny or herself. "You've never come to one and...I don't know...I just thought..."

He held up a hand to stop her. "Becs, look...I think you've got the wrong idea here. I'm not interested in going to some...bridal show. I mean...why would I?"

Her shoulders sagged and she gave him a patient smile as she reached for one of his hands. "Danny, this is something that's really important to me. I've been doing this since...forever! I tell you about these shows all the time and it would really mean a lot to me if you came and saw me model."

The loud bark of laughter was not was Becca was expecting.

At all.

"Um...Danny?" But when he continued to laugh, Becca pulled her hand away and began to nervously look around the parking lot. There weren't many people around at the moment—a couple of the florist trucks were parked by the curb and the delivery guys were too busy moving flower arrangements around to notice Becca and Danny—and there was some hipster-looking guy standing on the sidewalk checking something on his phone.

Clearing her throat, Becca took a step back and glared. "I don't see what's so funny about this," she said defensively, her arms crossing over her middle.

Danny McDowell had been Becca's ideal guy since the tenth grade. Of course back in high school, he never paid any attention to her. When they'd run into one another at a club six months ago and Danny asked for her phone number, Becca thought she'd died and gone to heaven. She knew part of it was because she looked a heck of a lot better at twenty-five than she had at sixteen—she had more confidence and had lost some of the weight that haunted her all through high school. Just thinking about how excited she'd felt when Danny actually approached her still made her a little giddy.

As time went on, however, she sort of found herself finding all kinds of things that really irritated her about him. Things she never really noticed back in school—he was extremely self-centered, kind of a loud-mouth, and he never wanted to do anything Becca did.

For a while she thought she could let it go, but tonight's show was important to her. Enchanted Bridal was celebrating their twentieth anniversary and it was something she had wanted to share with Danny. And she thought he'd want to share with her!

"Come on, Danny," she began, "you know why this is a big deal for me. Mrs. James is like a second mom to me and Hailey, Angie, Ella, and I have been in every show since the beginning. We're going to celebrate afterwards—cake and champagne and…it's going to be great." She reached for his hand and gave him what she hoped was a sexy smile. "I really want you there with me."

He sighed loudly and pulled his hand away before he walked around her and started to head back to his car. Becca frowned and went after him. The florist vans were pulling away and only the hipster was still around. When she caught up with Danny, she did her best to keep her voice down as she tried to figure out what was going on.

"Um…excuse me," she said. "But I'm standing here talking to you and you just walk away? What's going on, Danny?"

Stopping and spinning around, Danny raked a hand through his dark hair and stared down at her. He was easily six inches taller than Becca and normally it was something she loved, his looking down into hers. But right now, there was nothing sweet or sexy about his expression.

"Look, Becs," he began, and none too softly. "I really have no desire to stand around with a bunch of losers who are looking to give up the single life. It's a Friday night, for Christ's sake! I'm meeting the guys down at BJ's, I'm not hanging around while you parade around in a costume."

She took a step back as if he'd slapped her. "A costume? Danny, I model wedding gowns! This isn't some little game; it's a fashion show. A real fashion show!"

He snickered again. "Come on…you're kidding right?"

"What's that supposed to mean?" she demanded.

"Becs, you are no model. I mean…look at you. You're short, you're not thin and…well…" he waved his arms around to pretty much indicate her entire body. "You're just not model material." He shrugged. "The only reason you're in these shows is because you're friends with Hailey. There's no way anyone would actually choose you to be a model. Come on, blow this thing off and come to BJ's with me. I'll even let you win at darts."

Cars were starting to pull into the parking lot and for all the open space, Becca felt very closed in. "I'm not going anywhere with you," she hissed. "I'm serious, Danny. I can't believe you could say those things to me! I thought I meant something to you! I thought this was going somewhere!"

He laughed one more time. "You do mean something to me, Becs. You're fun. We've had

some good times and the sex has been great but…"

But?! There was a but?! She inwardly seethed.

"But this was never going to go beyond that. I thought you realized that. I'm not looking for anything serious and…well…if I were, you just aren't my type." He shrugged and pulled his keys out of his pockets.

"Not your type? How can you even say that?" she cried. "For months we've been sleeping together and you didn't seem to mind…my type!"

He gave her another shrug and managed to look bored before his gaze landed on her chest. "What can I say? I'm a breast man." And before Becca could even respond, Danny walked around to the driver's side of the car and unlocked it. "It's been fun, Becs, but…you know. I thought you understood."

"Danny…"

"Later," he said as he climbed into the car.

Becca stood there and watched him drive away as tears welled in her eyes. When his taillights were out of sight, she let the tears fall for a minute before wiping them away. That was it? She'd invested six months with him and all that time he was only interested in her because of…because of her bra size? Becca's mind raced with all of the degrading things he'd said and she felt like she was going to be sick.

Slowly she walked over to the sidewalk and sat

down on the lone wooden bench. The parking lot belonged almost solely to Enchanted, so the only traffic coming and going was from the vendors for the show tonight. Hugging her middle, she bent forward and forced herself to breathe.

All of the excitement she'd been feeling about the show and the party and the anniversary was gone. Right now all she wanted to do was get in her car, drive home and curl up in the fetal position. God, was she so hideous that the only reason a guy would sleep with her was because she had big boobs? Is that what all her other boyfriends had thought?

Every insecurity she'd ever had was now spinning around in her head, mocking her. Becca had no disillusions about herself—she wasn't classically beautiful like Hailey, or tall and glamorous like Angie. Hell, she wasn't even girl-next-door cute like Ella. But hey, it didn't make her some sort of troll either! And in her entire life, no one had ever said she wasn't pretty enough to model in the bridal shows.

The only reason you're in these shows is because you're friends with Hailey.

Oh, God. What if it was true? What if Mrs. James was losing business because Becca was an ugly bride?

Glancing around, she noticed the girls weren't there yet. If she could just get herself together, she could be out of here before they arrived and then call in sick. No one would have to know. There were no witnesses to her ever having been here! Part of her felt a little guilty because it was hard when a model didn't show up, but they'd dealt with it before and she knew Mrs. James would be able to make it work if she weren't there.

Scooping up her purse, Becca fished out her keys, stood up and wiped away the stray tears. She made it all of two steps before she tripped over her own feet and fell down on the pavement.

"Shit!" she cried. "Can I seriously not get a freaking break here?"

"Hey, are you all right?"

Oh great. The hipster.

"Yeah," she murmured. "I'm fine." Becca was surprised when he helped her to her feet and then bent over to pick up her purse and the items that had spilled out of it. When he stood back up and held her purse out to her, she was at a loss for words.

He was tall—not taller than Danny though—with the bluest eyes she had ever seen. He was wearing a knit beanie and from what she could see, his hair was a sandy shade of brown. He wore glasses and it should have made him look a little nerdy, but it didn't. With a strong jaw lightly shaded with stubble and...yes...dimples...he was almost breathtaking.

With a shaky hand she took her purse from him. "Um...thank you."

"Are you sure you're okay?"

"What? Oh...yeah. Fine. It wasn't that bad of a fall. I'm more embarrassed than anything else."

"You seemed pretty upset," he said softly. "You know…before the fall."

Great. He'd seen that too. "I guess I'm just not having a very good night."

He nodded. "Sorry about that."

Becca wasn't sure what she was supposed to say

or do, but she really did want to escape before the girls got there. "I…um…I really need to go," she said, carefully stepping off the curb and inching in the direction of her car. "Have a nice night." With a small wave, she spun around and went to walk away.

"He was wrong, you know."

Stopping in her tracks, Becca turned back around. "Excuse me?"

"That guy? The one who made you cry? I'm guessing he was your boyfriend or something, but whoever he was, he was wrong about you."

Stepping back toward him, Becca wasn't sure if she should graciously thank him or if she should be pissed at how he'd been listening.

She opted for pissed—with a hint of embarrassment.

"You were eavesdropping?" she asked incredulously.

He at least had the good sense to look embarrassed too. "It was kind of hard not to. You were standing right there."

Even though she knew he had a point, it still irked her. "Yeah, well…you shouldn't have. And you didn't need to let me know that you did."

This time he took a step toward her. "Look, maybe I shouldn't have said anything. But I stood here and watched you cry and I knew it was because of what he said and I…I just couldn't let you leave here believing anything he said."

"What difference does it make to you?" she snapped. "You don't even know me! How could you possibly say Danny was wrong?"

"Because I have eyes!" There was a hint of amusement in his tone. "I don't have to know you to see that you're a beautiful woman. And I highly doubt Mrs. James would let anyone model in her shows just because she felt an obligation!" He took a steadying breath before continuing. "Look, guys like that, they get off on putting other people down and it just ticks me off. There was no way I could just stand here and let you go home and cry some more because of that jerk. You were going to blow off the show and probably fake being sick or something and that's not fair. Not to you. And not to Mrs. James."

"How…how did you know that was what I was doing?"

He gave her a lopsided grin. "Really?"

196

She sighed and avoided meeting his gaze. "Okay, fine. That's what I was doing. But can you blame me? I was just dumped by my boyfriend in the middle of a parking lot after being insulted in every possible way! I think I kind of deserve a little time off to lick my wounds."

He shrugged. "Maybe. But that's just giving him the power back. It's letting him win. And believe me, guys like him do *not* deserve to win."

Now it was Becca's turn to chuckle. "You sound as wounded as I am. Did some jerk dump you today too?" He smiled. And Becca almost sighed at the sight of it.

"I'm Max, by the way," he said, holding out his hand to her.

"Becca." She put her hand in his and liked how big and firm his hand was. She smiled and gently took her hand back. "I think I'm still gonna bail. I'm not feeling very festive and I'm really not in the mood for any more witnesses to my humiliating night."

"My lips are sealed."

"Thanks." She paused. "How do you know Mrs. James?"

"I don't. I mean I do. Sort of. We just met a couple of days ago."

Becca looked at him in confusion. "But...just a minute ago you said..."

"I've heard a lot about her. And I still firmly believe she wouldn't have you in her shows, representing her business, if she didn't want you there."

"Oh." With a sigh of resignation, Becca was just about to wish him a goodnight when she heard voices behind her. A quick glance showed her it was too late to run and hide. When she looked back at Max, she saw the knowing grin on his face. "Dammit," she murmured.

"Don't look at it as a bad thing. No one's going to know what happened here unless you want to tell them."

While she knew he was right, she knew that as soon as everyone was here, they were going to talk about it—because it's what they always did. She had no secrets from her friends. Never had. And while she hated how Max had witnessed the entire scene with Danny, there wasn't anything she could do about it. The only upside was that she'd most likely never see him again.

"I should go," Becca said quietly. "The girls are all pulling up."

Max nodded. "I hope you have a good night, Becca. Go out there and have fun and don't let anything that jerk said ruin it for you."

"Thanks, Max," she said. "Have a good night, too."

This time when she turned and walked away, she did make it across the parking lot. Angie was the first to arrive and, as usual, Becca couldn't help but feel a little inferior to her friend. She was tall and curvy and confident and had a take-no-prisoners attitude toward everything.

Becca only dreamed of being so brave.

"Oh my God," Angie said as she climbed out of her sporty convertible. "I swear, the traffic gets crazier and crazier all the time. What's the point of having a convertible that lets the wind blow through your hair when you can't drive at a speed that creates a damn breeze?" She reached out and hugged Becca. "I almost did donuts in the parking lot just to get out my frustration."

"That would have been something."

They were about to walk toward the building when Angie stopped and put her hand on Becca's arm. "What's going on? What's the matter with you?"

Busted.

"What are you talking about?"

Leaning in a little closer, Angie scanned her face. "Something happened. You've been crying. Come on, out with it."

"Dammit, Ange…"

"We could wait for the girls but it might help to vent a little out here first."

It was a blessing and a curse when people knew you so well, Becca thought. With a shaky breath she went into detail about how things had gone with Danny. When she was done she looked up at Angie—expecting to see some sympathy.

"And you're surprised by this…why?"

Okay, not sympathy.